Keepers of the Vault

Melody and Myth

Published by Clockwise Press Inc., 56 Aurora Heights Dr.,
Aurora, ON Canada L4G2W7

www.clockwisepress.com

christie@clockwisepress.com   solange@clockwisepress.com

10 9 8 7 6 5 4 3 2 1

Library and Archives Canada Cataloguing in Publication
Chan, Marty, author
Melody and myth / Marty Chan.
(Keepers of the vault ; 2)
Issued in print and electronic formats.
ISBN 978-1-988347-00-4 (paperback).
ISBN 978-1-988347-02-8 (pdf)
I. Title.
PS8555.H39244M44 2016   jC813'.54   C2016-905560-4
C2016-905561-2

Cover Art by Harlee Noble
Cover and Interior design by CommTech Unlimited
The text of this book is set in Open Dyslexia font.
Printed in Canada by Webcom

KEEPERS OF THE VAULT

MELODY AND MYTH

MARTY CHAN

CLOCKWISE
PRESS

Much thanks and love go to the people who helped make this book possible. Thank you to Wei Wong, Michelle Chan, Christie Harkin, Kate Harkin, and Solange Messier for making my dreams come true.

M.C.

1: Stolen Goods

"**E**w! I think I found the Monkey's Paw."

I held up a shrivelled hairy hand. Its gnarled fingers reminded me of the chicken feet my Lao Lao used to boil. Mr. Grimoire peered up from his clipboard, slid his glasses up the bridge of his nose, and squinted at the artefact.

"No. That's the Hand of Glory."

"You mean there's another disgusting hand in the Vault?" I tossed the hideous thing on a nearby oak table.

"Three to be exact."

On the other side of the oak table, Dylan joked, "One more and we could play the most disgusting version of Patty Cake ever."

I karate-chopped my forehead to form a fin. "Snark attack!"

"I'm here all Snark Week."

"Watch out for the Snarknado!"

"What are you two going on about?" Grimoire stuck his head out from behind a pile of boxes, glaring.

"Nothing, sir," Dylan quipped. "Just giving Kristina a *hand*."

I groaned.

"Come on, you have to *hand* it to me for trying."

"Too far, Dylan, too far."

Grimoire shook his head. "Let's try to work more and chatter less, shall we? Kristina, place the Hand of Glory with the fingers facing *east*. Thank you."

We resumed picking up the artefacts littered across the marble floor. I couldn't believe that right below was my school. Well, not quite. The Vault existed in an inter-dimensional space that doubled as the school's storage area. If you found the right entrance, you'd enter the Vault. The wrong entrance took you to the dusty fourth floor of my school.

Grimoire protected the collection of artefacts from the prying eyes of the public. Many of the antiques within the Vault were magical and potentially dangerous—a fact I'd learned the hard way. Just a few days ago, I had accidentally set free a djinn named Niram who lived in a lantern, and she nearly burned the building down in an attempt to murder me.

Grimoire tugged his black vest over his ample waistline. He held out his hand. Dylan placed the artefact on his palm. "Try not to play with the artefacts. You never know what you might unleash."

"Well, it doesn't look very dangerous."

"Do not underestimate Blackwell's Phantasm Ball. Have you ever heard of the Minotaur?"

"Half bull, half man," Dylan said.

Grimoire shook the globe three times. Suddenly, the Minotaur appeared in the room and roared. Dylan yelped and stumbled backward, grabbing my arm. The horned creature snorted and stamped its foot but did not charge.

The old man laughed. "You're perfectly safe. Shake this artefact and you can conjure any image you desire."

Dylan let go of me. "Yeah. Well. It wasn't *that* scary."

Grimoire held the globe out. "Care for another demonstration?"

"No. I'm good." Dylan said quickly, eyeing the Minotaur, which was still huffing at him. "Um, when will this monster go away?"

"When the snow settles in the globe," Grimoire said. "Ignore him. He won't bite."

"Do you know what Rebecca wanted?" I asked.

The Keeper of the Vault shrugged. "Not exactly. We'll have to see what she has taken before we can understand what she wanted."

"I still don't get why your old apprentice broke in. Couldn't she have just taken the stuff out while she was still working for you?"

Grimoire shrugged. "She began to behave oddly only in the last few weeks. She talked about wanting the world to see them. Most insistently. That's when I decided to employ security measures around the Vault."

"I guess they didn't work," I said, surveying the damage to the Vault.

"Well, at the beginning, they did. When Rebecca first tried to steal from me, she set off my alarms and confirmed my suspicions. She disappeared before I could question her further, but I hoped that was the end of the matter."

"Except you weren't counting on her to trick us into freeing Niram." I eyed the display case that housed my old smartphone, which now doubled as a prison for the djinn.

Dylan added, "And almost getting us killed in the process."

Grimoire placed a hand on my shoulder. "Still, if not for Rebecca's deceit, I wouldn't have found my new apprentices."

"You mean cleaning staff," I joked.

"Snark attack," Dylan shouted.

The old man flashed a mischievous smile. "A rose by another name still smells as sweet."

"Burn."

"Enough. Back to work," Grimoire ordered.

Several hours later, we had restored most of the collection. Eight of the display cases had been damaged. I found all the items belonging to five of them, but in the end, three artefacts were still missing: Dr. Von Himmel's music box, Aleister Crowley's *Book of Spells*, and the Yellow Emperor's Dragon Teeth.

"What can Rebecca do with those things?" Dylan asked.

Grimoire stroked his chin. "Nothing good. Nothing good at all. Aleister Crowley was an occultist: a warlock with a book of spells."

"You mean the eye-of-newt and flying-broomstick kind of spell book?" I asked.

"A little more advanced than that but, yes, you are basically correct."

Dylan let out a low whistle. "What about the Dragon Teeth? Let me guess—they belonged to a dragon."

Grimoire nodded. "The Yellow Emperor slayed the dragon who plagued the Middle Kingdom, and he took the creature's teeth as his trophy. Legend has it that if you plant the teeth in the earth, terracotta soldiers will spring up and serve you."

I scratched my head. "Wait a minute. A spell book and seeds to grow an army? Sounds like she's preparing for war."

"All she needs is a wicked soundtrack, like from Gears of War. Maybe that's what the music box is for," Dylan said.

"Dr. Von Himmel experimented with sounds in the 1800s. He believed musical notes played in the right order and combination could affect the human brain, and he applied his theory to his music box. They say whoever plays the instrument will control the minds of anyone who hears the enchanted melody."

"I'm starting to see why you don't want this stuff to get out to the public," I said. "Can you imagine what you could do with a box that controlled minds?"

Dylan shrugged. "First thing I'd do is make Mr. Carlton give me a better mark in language arts."

I smacked his arm. "I'm serious. We have to get those artefacts before Rebecca sells them."

"Who would want those things?"

Grimoire answered, "I crossed paths with a few collectors of these rare antiquities. Most want them for the historical value, but a handful of them are interested in their magical properties. Those people are the ones who concern me the most."

"Why?" I asked.

"Let me say, the world of collectors is rather... unsavoury. Those who seek these artefacts may have questionable morals when it comes to how they possess them and how they use them."

"How do you think she's going to get a hold of these buyers?" Dylan asked.

"Like everyone else," I answered. "On the Internet."

2: The Dark Web

I watched over my shoulder as Dylan browsed a classifieds website on his smartphone. No luck with Dr. Himmel's music box or Aleister Crowley's *Book of Spells*. When he entered Dragon's Teeth, a search entry popped up at the top of the list.

"I think I've got a hit."

"What?"

My friend read the entry aloud. "If you want to up your game, my Dragon's Teeth are to die for. Why roll the dice with anything else? You'll be invincible. Instant chat DM34912."

"Do you think that's Rebecca?" I asked.

"Anything is possible," Grimoire said.

"Not bad for our first try," Dylan said. "High five."

"Wait until we know for sure before you humble-brag," I said.

"Nothing humble about it. Don't leave me hanging, Kristina." He waved his hand in the air.

I ignored him. "Mr. Grimoire, should we check it out?"

"I'm uncomfortable with you two going on your own. I'll go with you."

Dylan shook his head. "We don't have to go anywhere. The seller left their chat handle."

He tapped his phone screen as he explained. "Chat means we can text the buyer. Watch."

He held up the screen to reveal his opening message: "Interested in Dragon Teeth."

A moment later, a reply appeared. "Magnificent."

Dylan typed. "Want to see them first before buying."

"You won't be able to put them down. Bring cash."

"How much? Not interested if the price is too high," Dylan typed and hit send.

A few minutes later, the answer came. "One hundred grand per artefact."

Dylan let out a low whistle. "That's some serious cashews."

"Say we're good for the money," I said. "The cost doesn't matter. We're not paying for them anyway."

"Will do." He typed, "Where do we meet?"

A pause then a final message: "Sending map location now."

The three of us crammed into an ancient Volkswagen bug, the car Grimoire had bought years before he became the Keeper of the Vault. The car reeked of old Chinese takeout and motor oil. I plugged my nose as he white-knuckled the steering wheel and inched the car onto the main street.

Dylan huddled in the back of the car. "Sir, you might want to step a little harder on the gas pedal. That's what makes us go faster."

"I'm just getting used to driving again."

"So cars existed when you were younger?" Dylan asked.

I laughed, but Grimoire apparently did not see the humour.

The rush-hour traffic in Edmonton slowed us down even more. At one point, I thought we might be able to get to our destination faster on foot, but I decided to keep that comment to myself.

Grimoire checked the rear-view mirror. "Go around if you're in a rush," he muttered at the massive pick-up truck that nearly French-kissed our car's bumper.

Finally, Grimoire turned off the main street and into a residential neighbourhood. Dylan let out a melodramatic *phew* while I unclenched my hand from the door handle. We rolled to a stop in front of a bungalow protected by lawn gnomes. Was this Rebecca's hideout? I started to doubt we had the right place.

Dylan didn't share my doubts. He crawled out from the back of the car and led the way up the path. He rapped on the door several times and stood back. Beside me, Grimoire reached into his jacket as if he were reaching for a weapon.

The door opened to reveal a greasy man in a plaid shirt and sweat pants that had clearly seen better days. His unruly beard looked like a trap for potato chips and cookie crumbs.

"Yeah?" he grunted. "What do you want?"

"We're here for the Dragon's Teeth."

The man wiped his beard and smiled. "Ah, yes. Before you may enter, answer my riddles three. I have eyes but cannot see."

"What?" I asked.

"What has eyes but cannot see?" The bearded man asked again. He crossed his arms and stood his ground in the doorway.

"I think we have the wrong place," I said.

Dylan waved his hand. "No, hold on. I think I got this. I love LARPing. Is it a potato?"

The man smiled. "Yes. A wise paladin. Now the second riddle."

I cut him off. "Look, we don't have time for this. Sorry to waste your time."

I turned with Grimoire and headed back to the car.

Dylan reluctantly followed. "Sorry, dude."

"But don't you want to see my Dragon's Teeth dice? They're custom made. Best dice in D&D. They're loaded. You'll roll an eighteen every time. Twenty bucks...no, fifteen!"

"Seriously? An eighteen?" Dylan turned around. "With a high roll like that, you'll be able to do maximum damage almost every time."

"Come on," I hissed. Now was not the time to be getting Dungeons and Dragons loaded dice.

Dylan hesitated. "Fine," he huffed and crawled into the car's back seat.

The seller called after us. "Ten—and that's my final offer!"

I jumped in the Volkswagen and slammed the door.

Back at the Vault, Grimoire sifted through a leather-bound planner while Dylan and I swept the remnants of broken glass from the floor.

Dylan leaned on his straw broom. "What are you looking for sir?"

Barely looking up from the book, the old man answered, "I met one collector at a conference and exchanged cards. What was her name? Lenore something or other. She told me she might contact me from time to time, but that I'd need her card in order to read any message she'd send me."

"Do you think Rebecca found the card and contacted her?"

"I doubt it. The odd thing about this card is that it has no phone number or email. Ah, here it is."

He held up a postcard.

"Let me see," I said.

The front of the card had just a name in gold lettering: Lenore Frobisher. I flipped the card around. A series of numbers and letters filled the back. Too long to be a web address.

"Dylan, can I borrow your phone?"

"What's wrong with yours? Oh right. It's occupied." He glanced at the display case with my smartphone inside.

"You still owe me a new one, Mr. Grimoire."

"Yes, I remember. I could drive to the nearest outlet and pick one up."

"Might be faster if we walked," I muttered. I started to punch the code into the browser address.

"Um, what are you doing, Kristina?" asked Dylan.

"Entering the web address."

"Good luck with that. You're not going to get anything."

"How do you know?"

"That's not an address. It's a public key."

"A what?"

He explained, "If you want to send messages without snoops reading them, you encrypt the messages. Put them in code. But you want the person who gets the message to be able to read it, so she needs a public key to decode the thing. I think this is one of those keys."

"How do you know about this?" Grimoire asked.

"Got a friend who knows a friend. Anyway, any messages from the collector would be nonsense until you used this public key to confirm you're the person who is supposed to receive the note. Then the message is unlocked."

"Lenore told me she'd initiate contact and relay instructions on how to contact her. I haven't received any messages. At least, I don't think I have."

He sauntered to a massive computer monitor and started up the ancient machine. We huddled around the dusty screen. Other than spam for hair growth products and grocery store specials, Grimoire had received no email from Lenore Frobisher or any interested buyers. Or any friends for that matter.

"Well, that's a dead end," I said.

Dylan smiled. "Maybe not. I think I might know how Rebecca would try to sell the artefacts."

"How?" I asked.

"Ever hear of Sleepy Hollow?"

Grimoire smiled. "Ah yes, the birthplace of the Headless Horseman and the unfortunate demise of Ichabod Crane."

"I remember that story," I said.

"It's no story," Grimoire said.

Dylan and I glanced at each other. "Are you serious?" I asked.

He smiled cryptically. "What is your version of Sleepy Hollow?"

"Well, it's a site on the web. But not the regular one. The Dark Web. Sleepy Hollow is an online black market for things you might not want others to know about."

"Okay, then let's search this Sleepy Hollow," Grimoire said.

"That's not so easy. We need a TOR. The Onion Router. It's a tool to let us connect with addresses that are hidden on the clear net. The regular Internet. TOR keeps the government snoops from spying on people using the Internet."

"I don't follow," the old man said.

"Think of it as an online version of your Vault. Only those who have permission can enter."

"How do you know about all of this?" I asked.

"A...friend. She might be able to help us search Sleepy Hollow for any listings of the stolen artefacts."

Grimoire stiffened. "I can't afford to tell more people about the Vault."

"Don't worry. The person I'm thinking of can keep under the radar and she doesn't ask questions."

Grimoire raised an eyebrow. "How and why would you associate with someone like this?"

"It's not that shady. I was in the cafeteria, grinding Overwatch to level up but it was taking forever. I was about to punch the computer when this girl came up and stopped me. Then she hacked the game and just like that, I got all the XP I needed. Turns out she has a soft spot for rage quitters. Found out later that she knows more than cheat codes. She knows all about backdoors. She can help, if the price is right."

"I have some funds set aside for emergencies. Does she prefer cash? I have some gold nuggets as well."

Dylan waved him off. "No, she only accepts bitcoin."

"What is that?"

"Digital cash. Virtual money."

"I'm afraid this is beyond my ability to

understand," Grimoire said. "I'll leave it to you to discuss price. Besides, I have to restore the display cases and reset the Vault back to its rightful order. I believe the Hand of Glory sat 5.4 metres southwest of the Golden Fleece." He wandered off.

We watched the Keeper of the Vault measure the precise distance between two cases.

"You game to talk to my friend Anji?"

"Sure, Dylan. Lead the way."

Turned out we didn't have to go too far. In fact, we didn't even have to leave the school. Dylan's contact was a ninth grader who huddled over her laptop in the library. Her fingers flew across the keyboard with blistering speed and accuracy. The back of her hands and wrists were covered with henna tattoos, which were barely noticeable against her caramel skin.

"Anji?" Dylan interrupted. "Got a second?"

Hypnotic eyes peered out from under her black bangs. "What do you want?"

"To do some business. We're looking for some things online."

"Type 'E' and 'Bay' and I'm sure you'll find whatever you need."

"No, that might attract too much attention. We're looking for something a bit more underground, if you get my drift."

Anji closed the shell of her laptop and glanced around the library. Nearly deserted. "Let me guess. You're on the hunt for some code so you can mess up an online game or two."

Dylan cracked a grin. "Trust me. Nothing like that. Learned my lesson the last time."

She raised an eyebrow. "You know my rules. No guns or drugs."

I interrupted. "We're looking for some rare objects that we think might be on Sleepy Hollow."

Anji rolled her eyes and opened her laptop. "Who's your pushy friend, Dylan?"

"Anji, Kristina. Kristina, Anji."

"Good to meet you," I said. "I like your tattoos."

She cocked her head to the side until I pointed to her hands. "Oh, these. My cousin got married over the weekend. Takes a while for the henna to wash out."

"They look great. So do you think you can help us?" I asked.

"Depends on what you're looking for and what you're willing to pay. And it'll have to be more than cheap compliments."

Dylan tugged on my arm before I could reply. "Maybe let me negotiate with Anji."

"Fine," I said.

I wandered to the other side of the library to

browse books. I couldn't hear them, but I could guess by Dylan's arm movements he was working hard to get Anji's price down. A few minutes later, she opened the laptop. Dylan jogged over to me.

"Anji said to give her a day or so and she'll see what she can come up with."

"She's a testy one."

"Oh, don't take it personally. She's more of a lurker in real life, but you can't shut up her posts when she gets into it. One word of warning: do *not* ever tell her Picard is a better *Star Trek* captain than Kirk."

"Original Kirk or new Kirk?" I said, cracking a grin.

"Duh. Original Kirk. Always original Kirk."

We headed back to the fourth floor to report our progress to Grimoire. The locked doors of the storage area kept other students out, but they were our entry point to the Vault. As Grimoire had instructed, I grabbed the lock that held the chain around the door handles and spun the combination dial to the fourteen, to the six, to the one, and then finally to the twenty-two. The new passcode would keep Rebecca out and let us in.

A bright light shone down from the ceiling above us, only now the ceiling was gone. A rush of wind greeted my face and my body lifted into the air. I reached out and grabbed Dylan's sweaty hand as we floated up to a dark hole. For a second, I thought my lunch and breakfast were going to spew out, but then I touched down on a solid marble floor.

My friend clapped like a seal. "Again, again."

I told Grimoire about our findings. He greeted the news with a smile, but his grin turned into a scowl when Dylan tried to explain to him how to set up Anji's payment with bitcoin.

"You mentioned this before. So she desires loose change only?"

"No, there are no coins."

"Then why call them bitcoin?"

"They're digital cash made from bits of code. They don't exist anywhere except on the Internet."

"Then how do you give them to her?"

"Well, I'll transfer them to her virtual wallet. It's sort of like an electronic bank account that you own instead of an actual bank. It stores the information about the bitcoin."

"Then she can spend them at any store?"

"Not exactly. But some stores do accept bitcoin as a currency. Or you can sell them for dollars."

"But you just said the coins aren't real coins."

Dylan's shoulders slumped as he sighed. "Let me try this again."

"You know what, guys?" I said. "It's getting late. I promised my mom I'd be home in time to make dinner for us. I'll see you tomorrow. Okay?"

Neither Dylan nor Grimoire waved. My friend tried once again to explain the concept of virtual money to the Vault Keeper as I headed out.

Back at the apartment, I tossed my backpack on the sofa, which also doubled as my bed. I couldn't wait until we had enough money to afford at least a two-bedroom apartment, but with Mom going back to school, we couldn't afford anything bigger. I strolled into the kitchen to cook supper. The phone rang. As soon as I heard the voice on the other end, I regretted answering.

"Hello?" I said.

"Kristina, it's me. Dad."

I breathed into the receiver but said nothing.

"How are you?" he asked.

I had plenty of words for the man who had abandoned Mom and me because he was having a mid-life crisis and wanted to work it out with some other woman. The anger stuck in the back of my throat and became a sullen silence.

"I know I haven't seen you much over this

last year, but I wanted to change that. I hoped we could get together this weekend and hang out."

Finally, I found my voice. "Why? You never bothered to see me before."

"I'm sorry about that, Kristina. I want to make it up to you. Can we start fresh?"

"Why?"

A pause. "I have tickets this weekend for the Oilers' game. Thought you might want to go."

"Hockey's your thing. Not mine."

"I have an extra ticket. Maybe you can bring one of your friends."

"Why? Are you bringing your *friend*?"

"No. It'll just be me."

I glared at the receiver, silently daring him to mention his friend.

"So, are you up for a weekend outing with your dad, Kristina?"

"You mean like all the other weekends you promised but never showed up?" I said.

"We don't have to watch hockey. We could do whatever you want. What do you say?"

He sounded almost apologetic. It was like he needed something and I was the only one who could give it to him.

Fine. Whatever he wanted, he'd have to work for it.

"The Acid Drones are playing on Friday," I said.

"I've never heard of the Acid Drones. What kind of music do they play?"

"Thrash metal."

"I didn't know you were into that kind of music."

I wasn't, but I knew he hated metal. "You want to spend time with me, that's what I want to do. Front row."

"Well. Okay. I'll see what I can scrounge up."

"And get an extra ticket for my boyfriend," I added. "Skull Crusher loves the Acid Drones. And if he gets a free ticket, he can save his money to get that new tongue stud."

"Um, Skull Crusher?"

I hung up on him. And when the phone rang again. I chose not to answer.

3: BAIT AND SWITCH

I didn't want to tell Mom about Dad asking to take me this weekend. She didn't need to know Dad was trying to weasel back into our lives. It's not like he would show up or anything. Instead, I curled up in my blanket and pretended to be asleep when she came home.

In truth, I didn't sleep much through the night. All I could think about was the moment my father walked out of my life, carrying a duct-taped red suitcase and a garment bag with his suit jackets. I called after him, but he didn't even bother to look back. Even in my dreams, I replayed that moment over and over again, until my alarm went off.

At school, I dealt with the aftermath of a sleepless night and a memory I wanted to erase from my mind.

"You okay, Kristina?" Dylan asked. "You look like some of the guys after an Overwatch marathon."

"Did you talk to Anji? Did she find anything?"

"I'm going to see her at lunch."

"What's taking her so long? She's good at

this, right? Maybe we should find someone else."

"Whoa. Easy there, Kristina. This kind of stuff takes time. We don't even know if Rebecca will post something on Sleepy Hollow. She might be using some other Dark Web site."

"Sorry, Dylan. Miserable weekend."

"What happened?"

"Nothing." I could talk to Dylan about a lot of things, but this wasn't one of them. Though divorced, both his parents still spent time with him. He wouldn't understand what I was going through.

"I'll see you at lunch, Dylan."

"Okay. Sure. What's bugging you?"

"Nothing." I walked away before he could ask any more questions.

Dylan and I met up at the library at noon. Anji had come through, but she wasn't going to spill anything until we paid. "I didn't see any bitcoin in my wallet."

"Yeah, I wanted to wait till I saw you so I could make sure I was transferring the right amount. The price of bitcoin has been going up lately."

He tapped on the screen of his phone.

A moment later, Anji's phone pinged. She checked her device and nodded. "Okay, now we can get down to business."

"What did you find?" I asked.

We settled into a table at the back of the library and Anji cracked open her laptop. "I'm not sure why someone's using the Dark Web for stuff like this. I'm going to assume it's worth a lot, and that it's stolen. Someone with the handle NewWorldOrder17 is trying to dump a music box. Claims it's an antique with an enchanted melody. Does that sound like what you're looking for?"

"Yes," I said. "Can we communicate with her?"

Anji typed and waited for a second. "Yes, she posted her public key. You can instant message her. What's the deal with a music box? If you are trying to buy stolen goods, the deal's off."

I glanced at Dylan. "I thought you said she wasn't going to ask questions."

"Oh, it's stolen all right. From Grimoire. We're trying to get it back. Beyond that, everything else is on a need-to-know basis."

She flashed a sneer at me for a second then forced a smile. "Of course. That's why I get the big bitcoin. I'll set up an instant message for you. Untraceable, I'm assuming?"

I nodded.

She typed on her keyboard. After a few minutes, she spun the laptop around.

"Secure?" Dylan asked.

"Do you even need to ask? Hit enter when you want to send the message. Don't worry, I'm not going to watch."

I stared at the girl, nudging Dylan.

"Uh, Anji, mind waiting over there?"

"Is this going to get me on the six o'clock news?"

He shook his said. "You'll be clean. Nothing to worry about."

"Okay, but give me your phone. I need to check my email and mine is out of juice."

He handed her his phone. Anji walked away, never taking her eyes off me.

"Okay, here's what we'll say, Dylan," I ordered. "Say you're interested in examining the piece to confirm it's real. You don't want to meet anywhere that will attract attention."

"Where do you want the meeting?" Dylan asked.

"Someplace where we can spring a trap on her. It will have to be a secluded area."

"We'll do it at night."

"A secluded spot in the evening. Maybe the Legislature Building. There's a park area in the back. No one would see us there."

He dismissed the idea. "No. Security roams the grounds. They chased me off last summer when I was boarding through the paths. We need a place where no one's going to stumble across us."

One spot sprang to my mind: the Chinese Garden where my grandmother had taken me many times. It was Lao Lao's favourite spot. Nestled in the river valley just south of the downtown skyscrapers, the small park featured a gazebo with a pagoda roof and statues of Chinese astrological symbols.

"How about the Chinese Garden?"

"Where is that?"

"Downtown river valley. The fact you don't know where it is says a lot about how secluded it is. I've been there dozens of times."

"Okay. We'll meet her there. I'll send the message."

He sent a chat message to NewWorldOrder17. A few seconds later, Anji's laptop pinged with a return message.

"*The music box isn't cheap. Do you have the money?*"

"What do we tell her, Kristina?"

"Say we have fifty grand, but will only pay if she has the real deal."

He typed the message and sent it.

A pause. Then a reply: "*I don't leave my*

room for less than 100K."

I chewed my bottom lip. "Tell her we'll bring 50K to look, and if it's what we want, she'll get another 50K."

He nodded. After what felt like forever, the screen finally lit up.

"Fine. Where?"

He typed, "Chinese Garden. Edmonton, Canada. How soon can you get into town?"

"Tomorrow night. Nine."

Dylan held up his hand for a high five. "She took the bait, Kristina."

I slapped his hand. "That one you earned."

We headed back to the fourth floor to report our findings. Grimoire nearly vibrated when we told him the news. "Excellent, just excellent. And you're sure this is Rebecca? I would prefer not to engage with another role player again. That young man reeked of sweat and luncheon meat."

"We won't know for sure until we see her," Dylan said. "But a music box selling for $100,000 probably isn't the one you'd find at a flea market."

"And anyone selling a music box on the Dark

Web is definitely someone who has something to hide," I argued.

Grimoire scowled. "I can't believe she would be this devious."

"People can change."

"Not my apprentices," he snapped.

"Mr. Grimoire, I know you're upset, but sometimes you don't know people as well as you think you do," I said.

Dylan added, "Right now, we need to figure out how to catch her."

"Ah, yes. My apologies. I lost my head for a moment. I might have something." The old man wandered away.

"Are we going to get a giant net and go all Wile E. Coyote on her?" Dylan joked.

"Who?" I asked.

"Wile E. Coyote. Old *Bugs Bunny* cartoons. I thought you were retro."

"Just video games. Not cartoons."

"Oh, Kristina, I have much to teach you," Dylan said.

Grimoire returned with a Mason jar filled with orange goop.

"What is that?" I asked.

"Beeswax. It will plug our ears in case she decides to use the music box on us."

"Where did you get that?"

"From Odysseus. He used this very substance against the Sirens when they tried to lure him to their rocky shores with their beautiful music."

"Odysseus? He's real?"

The old man nodded. "The only problem is we won't be able to hear each other once we apply the beeswax. We'll have to coordinate our attack. Rebecca will recognize me, so I'd better hide."

"She probably knows what I look like, too," I pointed out.

We turned to Dylan, who raised both hands. "Hold on. She saw me, too. I'm happy to help, but I like staying alive. Remember? Me... toasted marshmallow?"

"Of course. We'll give you a disguise. A hat perhaps. Don't worry, we'll be right behind you."

"Yeah, because that's the safest place to be, Mr. Grimoire."

The old man clapped a hand on my friend's shoulder. "Listen. You don't need to go through with this if you don't want to."

"I don't want to."

"But you're our best hope," I said. "All you have to do is keep her talking. Just stall her."

"What will you guys be doing?"

Grimoire headed to a drawer and retrieved a long bamboo pipe and a feathered dart. "I haven't used this since my safari days. I believe I'm still a fairly good shot with the blowpipe. A little curare on the tip and she'll be instantly paralyzed."

"And what if you miss?"

"He won't miss, right?" I nudged the old man. He inserted the projectile and placed the bamboo pipe to his lips and blew. The dart flew out with blistering speed and spiked a suit of armour in the chest.

"That was your target, right?" Dylan asked.

He shrugged. "More or less."

The next night, we arrived at the Chinese Garden two hours before the meeting. Mom would be in class so she wouldn't worry about me. Still, I left her a voice message to tell her I'd be hanging out at Dylan's house.

When I checked through the voicemails before I left, there were four messages from my father, but I deleted them all as soon as I heard his grating voice. Probably bailing on the weekend, as usual.

"Thanks," I said, handing Dylan's phone back to him. "Someday, I'll have a phone of my own again, right?"

The old man shrugged as I glared at him. "All in good time."

"Wait until Christmas. The new models come out then," Dylan said. He fished out a cord and portable battery from his backpack and plugged the phone into the black box. Then he set everything on the seat beside him.

Grimoire parked his Volkswagen at the top of the hill.

"We walk from here," I said.

We climbed out of the car. The night air was brisk. I warmed my hands under my armpit. Steam rose from Dylan's mouth as he gulped and spat out his breath in rapid succession. He reminded me of a shivering puppy.

We mapped out our plan. Grimoire and I would hide in the bushes behind the gazebo while Dylan waited under the awning. He would position himself so Grimoire had a clear shot at Rebecca when she showed up. We needed the best vantage point. Even though we were early, I wasn't taking any chances. I unscrewed the lid of the Mason jar and slathered my finger with the beeswax and coated my ear.

"She's not supposed to meet us for two hours," Grimoire pointed out.

"What?" I said. At this point I couldn't hear out of my left ear.

"Too soon. We need to be able to communicate with one another."

"Just testing. Don't want this stuff to fail when the time comes."

I slathered the beeswax into my other ear. The sudden silence reminded me of the pool and dunking my head under water. The word *peaceful* came to mind.

Grimoire tried to say something, but I couldn't hear anything. He finally pointed at himself and Dylan and made a walking motion with his fingers toward the gazebo a hundred feet away.

"Okay," I yelled, but I couldn't hear my own voice.

At the bottom of the stairs, the stone bridge and small pond awaited me. I walked to the bridge and placed my hands on the cool stone, imagining my grandmother standing beside me. We used to stand here on Sundays in the summer while she explained how the garden honoured the Chinese immigrants who had come to Canada to help build the railroad.

I glanced back at my companions. Dylan adjusted a wide-brimmed hat to cover his face while Grimoire counted the steps between the gazebo and some nearby bushes.

I crossed the bridge to examine the tiny rat statue on the other side. I always asked Lao Lao why the cat had no statue. She told me Buddha hosted a race to figure out which animals would make up the astrological calendar. Too small to outrun the other animals, the rat and the cat agreed to ride on the back of an ox. The cat bragged he'd be the first one to finish and the rat decided to play a trick on the too-proud feline. When they neared the finish line, the rat pushed the cat off the ox's back and won the race. The other animals took the remaining eleven spots, leaving the cat out of Buddha's favour, and cats have hated rats ever since. I would make her tell this folktale again and again.

I sighed, remembering how I used to welcome those Sunday visits as if they were Christmas mornings. I missed her stories.

Back at the gazebo, something seemed off. Dylan stood in the centre, ramrod straight. Outside, Grimoire raised the blowpipe to his mouth and fired a dart at Dylan's chest. My friend crumpled to the ground. A woman in a long black coat stepped out from behind the bushes. She clutched a music box as she approached the Keeper of the Vault.

Rebecca.

4: Ambushed

I retreated behind the stone bridge, hoping Rebecca hadn't seen me. I couldn't hear what she was saying to Grimoire, and I debated whether or not to clear the wax out of my ears. When she pocketed the music box, I thought it might be safe. I jammed my fingers into my ears and scraped out the goo.

The shrill voice of Rebecca filled the night air. "You must obey me, old man. We're going to find your crappy excuse for a car, then you're going to take me back inside the Vault and give me the Golden Fleece."

Grimoire dropped the blowpipe on the ground and walked to the wooden staircase. I ducked low, waiting for them to pass. When I heard their footsteps on the wood, I got up and rushed to the gazebo to check on Dylan. His eyes were open and he was breathing. I pulled the dart out of his chest.

"Hang in there, Dylan."

I picked up the blowpipe from behind the gazebo. I'd only have one shot at this, but I hoped some curare still coated the tip. I sprinted up the hill, scrambling through the bushes, hoping to catch up to Grimoire and Rebecca.

They stood beside his car. I crouched behind a bush near the top of the hill, straining to hear them.

"You never clean this car. I always hated that about you," Rebecca said. "You should order your new apprentices to do it. Speaking of which, where is the other one?"

Grimoire struggled and shook his head.

"Tell me where she is."

Finally, he spoke. "She's waiting to ambush you down the hill."

She turned to look. I ducked back, afraid she might see me. She grabbed the crank on the music box and began to turn it. I slid down the hill, belly first, jamming my fingers into my ears, hoping they'd block the music. As the rough ground scraped against my legs, all I could hear was my own panting. Finally, I came to a stop about halfway down. I counted to three silently then gingerly pulled my hands away from my ears. No music.

"If you can hear the sound of my voice, I command you to come out and show yourself," Rebecca shouted from a distance.

I felt no urge to obey her.

"Oh, hello. And who might you be?" Rebecca asked.

"Anji."

My eyes widened. I climbed back to the top of the hill and peered through the bush. Dylan's hacker friend had now joined Rebecca and Grimoire.

"What are you doing here?" Rebecca asked.

"I was curious about what Dylan and Kristina were up to. I didn't want their dirty trail to lead back to me."

Rebecca laughed. "Well, you can do me a favour and clean up that dirty trail. Make sure Dylan and Kristina stay right here. Do whatever you think is necessary."

Anji nodded.

Rebecca turned to Grimoire. "Give me the keys. The last thing I want is for you to drive. I'll be your age by the time we get there."

Grimoire fished in his pocket for the keys. My only chance. I knelt as I inserted the feathered dart into the end of the pipe and placed the other end in my mouth. I inhaled through my nose and blew air out through the blowpipe as if I were clearing out a snorkel. The dart zipped out. Target: Rebecca's thigh.

Bullseye! She yelped in pain as she reached down to pluck the dart from her leg. She began to tip over to one side, grabbing Grimoire for support. The music box dangled from her other hand.

I sprinted toward the group. Grimoire and Anji were too focused on Rebecca to notice me.

"The car keys," Rebecca mumbled, trying to stay upright. "Now."

He gave Rebecca the keys. I closed the gap. Rebecca looked up and spotted me. She grabbed Anji by the jacket. "S-s-stop her," she stammered.

Anji began to turn as I slammed into her, shoving her into Rebecca and Grimoire. The music box fell to the ground while Rebecca staggered back with the car keys. I scooped up the music box just as Anji grabbed my arm.

Rebecca staggered to the car and fumbled with the keys to open the door. "Grimoire, bring me the music box."

The Vault Keeper lurched toward me like a zombie unleashed. I tried to pull away, but Anji had too strong a hold on my arm. My hand slipped from the top of the box to the crank handle. I tried to turn it, but I couldn't get a decent grip on it. Straining against Anji's hold, I just managed to nudge the crank. Two notes chimed out and the grip on me loosened.

"What's going on?" Anji asked in a daze.

Grimoire stopped in his tracks.

I pushed her away and bent down to grab the music box, but someone shoved me from behind, toppling me over.

"That's-s-s mine," Rebecca slurred.

She bent down to pick up the box. I rolled to my feet and charged at her before she could turn the crank, but she slipped out from under my grasp and hobbled to the car. I chased after her. She grabbed the stunned Grimoire and pushed him at me, forcing me to step around. Rebecca jumped into the car and locked the door. I covered my ears and backed away. She turned the music box crank, but I heard nothing.

Suddenly, the Volkswagen lurched toward me, picking up speed. She was going to run me down.

I froze. Grimoire grabbed my arm and yanked me out of the way. The car swerved at us, hitting the curb instead. The hubcap screeched against the cement and popped off, rattling down the street while the car fishtailed and roared off into the night.

Anji wavered on her feet. "What is going on? It was like I couldn't do anything but listen to her. I was trapped in my own head. Who's the old man?"

"This has nothing to do with you, Anji. Mr. Grimoire, are you all right?"

Anji grabbed my arm. "I want some answers."

"I don't have to tell you a thing."

"You do if you want to find the woman with that music box."

Grimoire shook off the effects of the spell.

"Where's Rebecca?"

"She got away," I said.

"And who is this?"

Anji answered. "I'm the person who can track her down."

"What? How?" I asked.

"I was worried Dylan was getting into something he couldn't get out of, so when I had his phone, I hacked the GPS locator so I could find you. I tracked his phone right to your car and it's still in there. So if you want to find your music box and that strange woman, I'm the only one who can help you figure out where that car went. But I'm not going to do anything until you tell me what this is all about."

Grimoire and I exchanged looks. "How badly do you want the music box back?" I asked.

"Tell her."

"You're sure?"

"We could use the help."

"Okay, sir." I turned to Anji. "You're going to have trouble believing this at first, but trust me it's the truth."

"After that weird thing with the music box, I'm prepared to believe anything."

"I'll explain but we have to check on Dylan first." I headed down the steps with Grimoire and Anji.

Dylan's eyes were wide open and his mouth was frozen in a grimace. His chest rose and fell, so I knew he could breathe.

Grimoire explained. "The curare is doing its job. I'm afraid it will be a few hours before he can move again. Sorry, Dylan."

Dylan let out a pathetic squeal as his eyes shifted to Anji.

"She was following us," I said. Then I explained everything: the secret vault at the top of the school, the collection of curses and magical items Grimoire had collected over the years, and Rebecca's role in the whole mess.

"I've never seen anything like that at the top of the school," Anji said.

"The fourth floor is actually a portal entrance rather than the actual Vault," Grimoire explained. "Think of it as a secret doorway."

"How did you guys find it?"

"We think Rebecca, the woman with the music box, might have secretly helped Kristina and Dylan find the door."

"What for?"

I answered, "So she could distract Mr. Grimoire and sneak into the Vault to steal the music box and some other items. And if we don't catch her, she's going to use those artefacts. I'm not sure how or on whom, but based on tonight, I can tell you that it won't be to help people."

Anji fished out her smartphone and tapped the screen, opening an app. Within a minute, she had pinged the location of Dylan's phone.

"Here you go." She showed me the screen, which flashed a city map and a blue dot crawling through the streets.

I beamed. Finally, things were looking up.

"Let's get Dylan back to the Vault," Grimoire said. "Now that we can track Rebecca, we can regroup and sort out a plan of attack."

I nodded. We carried Dylan to the top of the hill and Anji called a car share service to pick us up.

Back in the Vault, while we waited for Dylan to recover, Anji marvelled at the artefacts. She had about a million questions: "How did we not know this place was at the top of our school? Where are we really? How did you get all of this awesome stuff?"

Grimoire beamed. "I like this girl. She has an appreciation for the finer things."

"Why is Rebecca so interested in the Golden Fleece?" I asked.

"You've heard the legend, haven't you?"

"In grade six, my teacher talked about Jason going after the Fleece. I think he had to get past a serpent or something. After that, I can't remember."

Anji piped up. "Jason's uncle tricked him into getting the Golden Fleece. Jason thought he'd become the king of Iolcus if he got the artefact, but the uncle knew that any mortal who tried had died a horrible death. Jason sailed through the clashing rocks of the Symplegades, fought off harpies, and yoked two fire-breathing iron oxen before he reached the serpent guardian and the prize."

"Whoa. How do you know all that?" I asked.

"I must have had a better grade six teacher than you."

I rolled my eyes at her then turned to Grimoire. "What happened after he got the Golden Fleece?"

"Tragic consequences. Jason never claimed the throne of Iolcus nor did he live to a ripe old age. He died when a piece of his ship's timber struck him in the head. I swear this thing brings only misery."

"What does the Golden Fleece actually do?" Anji asked.

"Can you imagine having something that would make you immortal? It has the power to heal wounds and cure diseases. Some say it can cheat death. There are people who would pay anything for that gift. Rebecca could sell the Golden Fleece for any price."

"No way anything can be that powerful," Anji said.

"Can we see it?" I asked.

"Turn away and close your eyes," he ordered.

Anji and I obeyed. After a minute I decided to peek. I squinted at the reflection of Grimoire in the glass display just ahead of me. He navigated an invisible maze, thrusting his hands out every now and then until he reached the pedestal and snapped his fingers three times. A low hum filled the air for a second and then the Golden Fleece materialized before Grimoire. He picked up the pelt and walked over to us. The curled horns of the ram's head were striking, but not as mesmerizing as its deep blue eyes. The Golden Fleece twinkled like tinsel on a Christmas tree.

He spun around.

"You can look now."

We turned.

"So this is what the fuss is about." Anji eyed it critically. "Looks like something you'd see in a hunting lodge."

"Trust me, Anji. This is one of the most valued artefacts in the entire collection. I had hoped Rebecca would protect it with her life; instead, she has proven herself a thief and a traitor. I thought I could trust her."

"What made you think you could trust her?"

Anji asked. "Trust no one: That's what I always say."

"I've tried out many apprentices over the years, but none seemed to have the right qualities until Rebecca came along. From time to time, I would take on a janitorial position at the school whenever I needed to scout out new apprentice candidates. Rebecca never seemed to enjoy the company of others and spent most of her breaks and lunches on the stairs leading to the fourth floor. I saw potential in her and began to keep an eye on her."

"Was she shy or just anti-social?" I asked.

"I suspect she didn't have a lot in common with her classmates. She was orphaned at three. Her parents died in a car accident, and the duty of raising her fell to her grandmother. When she was a teenager, she had a falling out with the old woman and ran away. I don't know why, but Rebecca decided she wanted to get away from the only family she ever knew. She even lived on the streets for a time. Eventually, Rebecca ended up in a foster home and attended school here."

"What did she do that made you think she deserved the apprenticeship?"

"Ah, well," Grimoire smiled slightly at the memory. "A boy had been accused of stealing something from one of the popular girls. I don't know if there was any truth to the accusation, but as these things go, the truth didn't matter. He earned a reputation, and the students were merciless with him. Verbal abuse, pranks, and sometimes even physical violence. Only Rebecca befriended him. She stood up for him when the others turned on him. Her lone voice didn't matter to the others, but she still spoke up for him. In the end, they both became outcasts, but I knew she had a good heart."

Dylan's groans interrupted Grimoire's storytime.

"I... told... you.... this was a bad idea," he moaned.

"You'll be fine," Grimoire said, turning and helping him to his feet.

Anji asked, "If this Rebecca is onto you, are you in danger?"

Grimoire nodded. "I'm afraid so."

"But we know what she wants," I said. "As long as the Golden Fleece's here, we have nothing to worry about."

"You're sure she can't get in here?" Dylan asked.

"Yes. Nevertheless, this weekend, I'll double the security."

"Then what do we do in the meantime?" I

asked. "Are we just going to wait for her to try to break in?"

Anji shook her head. "We can track her." She eyed her phone. "Looks like she's stopped now. Somewhere on the city's north end. We could go now."

"Not until we are better prepared. We know what she can do with the music box, and I do not want a repeat of tonight."

Dylan yawned. "I don't know about you, but I could use the time to recover. Not every day a guy gets poisoned. I'd better call my mom and tell her I'm on my way."

"Um, Dylan, about your phone," I said. "Rebecca stole the car and your phone was still in the back seat."

"Oh man, I had everything in there!"

Anji leaned over. "If you have everything on the cloud, you should be safe."

He moaned. "Why didn't I take the time to do that?"

She patted his back. "Don't worry. We find her, we find your phone."

"Mr. Grimoire, I'll come tomorrow and help you beef up the safeguards," I offered.

"No. You'll just get in my way."

"At the very least, let me watch. I'll need to learn this stuff eventually, won't I?"

"Just make sure our new ally keeps quiet about everything," he said, eyeing Anji.

"You don't have to worry about me," she said. "I know how to lock things down."

He smiled, but flashed me a warning look. I nodded. "I'll keep an eye on her. Can I borrow your phone, Anji?"

She tossed me her device and I called Mom.

To say Mom wasn't happy would have been an understatement. She was furious.

"Your father showed up to pick you up this weekend. He claims you set this up. Get home. Now."

She hung up before I could say anything.

"Trouble?" Dylan asked.

"You don't know the half of it. We'd better get going."

"Wait, I have something for you," Grimoire called after us. He strolled to Tabula Rasa and chipped off pieces from the stone tablet. He handed us the rock chips.

"What's this?"

"You've heard of the Rosetta stone, haven't you?"

I shook my head.

"Archaeologists uncovered a stone that contained a decree from King Ptolemy the Fifth. His orders were etched in three languages: Greek,

Demotic and Egyptian hieroglyphs. The stone helped the archaeologists decode and understand Egyptian writing."

"This is the stone?"

"No, but this slate appeared in the same temple. I present to you, Tabula Rasa."

"What does the thing do?" Dylan asked.

"In short, the slate is like an ancient phone that receives texts."

"Wouldn't it be easier just to buy me a replacement phone?" I asked.

He shook his head. "Chip a piece off the rock and you can etch a message on any surface anywhere. Whatever you etch will appear on the tablet. In case you see Rebecca, you can contact me. Just write a message with the rock chip and I'll see the note on the slate."

"Do you think Rebecca will be after us?" Dylan asked.

"Better safe than sorry," Grimoire answered. "Now, go on home. I have work to do."

He stroked the Golden Fleece and watched us leave. I wondered if he was making sure that we couldn't see where he was going to hide it. He didn't trust us to see the security system for the artefact or its hiding place. Maybe he didn't trust Anji, but I thought he trusted Dylan and me. Either we hadn't earned his respect or he thought we'd turn on him like Rebecca did. Whatever the reason, Grimoire was being extra careful.

"Fine," I said. "We'll see you after the weekend."

5: FATHER TIME

O n the bus ride home, I half-hoped the vehicle would break down and I would be so late my parents would give up waiting. No such luck. Dad sat on the sofa nursing a bottle of beer while Mom leaned against the wall, arms folded, and glaring at him. Lao Lao's story about the rat and cat sprang to mind, but I couldn't tell if Mom was the cat or the rat.

"Where have you been?" Mom demanded.

"I called. I was hanging out with Dylan."

"Why didn't you tell me Dad called you?"

"Slipped my mind, I guess."

Dad put his beer on the coffee table. "Kristina, you know I was supposed to pick you up tonight. I got the tickets to the concert you wanted. I don't like being stood up."

"Well, now you know how it feels," I shot back.

Mom cut me off. "I don't know what you've been up to, but I'm not letting you hang around with some guy named Skull Crusher."

"Who?"

Dad pulled out tickets from his shirt pocket.

"The friend you wanted the extra ticket for. Skull Crusher."

"Oh," I said. I hadn't expected my lie to grow legs and run into Mom.

"Well?" she asked. "Who is this guy?"

"I was messing with Dad. I didn't think he was actually going to show up."

"These tickets weren't cheap, you know," he said.

I shrugged. "So?"

He glared at me, but said nothing. Mom, on the other hand, had a few choice words. "This is unacceptable, Kristina. I don't care what or how you feel about your father, you do not shirk your responsibilities."

"But, Mom..."

"No excuses. I didn't raise my daughter to bail whenever she doesn't want to do something."

Ouch. In getting back at Dad, I realized, I had acted exactly like him. "Sorry," I mumbled.

She crossed her arms. "I packed your suitcase, Kristina. You get to spend the rest of the weekend with your father."

"What? You're punishing me?"

"No, I'm making you stand by your obligations." She looked past me at Dad.

"I don't really think spending time with me is

all that bad," he protested.

"I wouldn't know," I said.

"Just go with your father," Mom said. "You made a *promise*. Stick with it."

The way she said *promise* made Dad flinch this time. Ouch, again.

Dad picked up my suitcase. "Let's go, Kristina."

If glares could kill, I would have murdered Dad with mine. Instead, I grabbed my suitcase from him and walked to the door.

"I'll see you Sunday," Mom called after me.

Too mad to answer, I stomped out. If Dad was going to make my life miserable, I planned to return the favour.

The rest of the weekend played out like the most boring movie Hollywood had ever made.

DAD: You want lunch, Kristina?

ME: I don't care.

DAD: Want to watch the hockey game with me?

ME: I don't care.

DAD: How about we go for a walk in the river valley like we used to?

ME: Too cold.

DAD: How about takeout dim sum? You still love the turnip cake, right?

ME: Not hungry.

DAD: How about you tell me what you want to do?

ME: Nothing.

DAD: Do you want to talk about anything? I'm here for you.

ME: Do you want to talk about the woman you were dating behind Mom's back?

We repeated a version of this conversation through breakfast, lunch, and supper. Around Sunday morning, my father gave up and we settled into an awkward silence. On the ride back to my real home, he tried one more time to spark a conversation. "I know this has been difficult for you, Kristina. It's been hard on all of us. Your mom and I, we didn't click anymore. It had nothing to do with you."

I stared at the red tassel of the miniature Chinese lantern that hung from his rear-view mirror, refusing to give him any room to squeeze in his lame explanation for leaving the family.

"Sometimes, I forget how much you've grown, Kristina. Seems like yesterday I was holding on to the back of your bicycle seat while you were wobbling down the sidewalk."

"What do you want, Dad?" I said.

"I thought we could start over. Be friends again."

"I'll make it simple for you. I have enough

friends and I'm not looking to add you."

"Kristina, I don't know how to reach you now."

"Maybe that's because when you forgot how to be Mom's husband, you also forgot how to be my dad."

He gripped his steering wheel and stared straight ahead for a few moments. His face flushed red and his jaw tensed. The rest of the trip was funeral-home silent. When we reached the apartment building, I hopped out before he could roll to a full stop. I grabbed my suitcase from the back and slammed the door shut. Without looking back, I headed into the building. The squeal of tires meant Dad wasn't waiting until I got in.

When I walked into the apartment, Mom was studying at the kitchen table. "How was your weekend?" she asked.

"How do you think it went?" I said.

"Look at what I picked up from Noodle Noodle."

She opened the fridge and pulled out Styrofoam containers of dim sum dishes, including my favourite: turnip cake.

I was still fuming over what she had done to me, and I didn't want to let her off the hook. I glared at the containers and lied. "I'm not hungry."

"I can't fry the turnip cake the way Lao Lao used to, but this is the next best thing."

She cleared away her textbook and set the container on the table. "Maybe for later, when you're hungry. Good night." She grabbed her books and headed into her room.

After she was gone, I pulled chopsticks out of the kitchen drawer and attacked the leftover dim sum. I sawed a piece of the softly fried turnip cake in half, picked up a piece, and dipped it in soy sauce before I popped it in my mouth. Soft and crunchy at the same time. A perfect balance of tastes and textures. Not quite as good as Lao Lao's, but I still enjoyed it. No doubt, this was Mom's way of bribing her way into my good books. It was a cheap tactic, but with every bite I took, I realized it was working.

I couldn't stay mad at her. If I had told her about Dad's call, she would have probably told him to disappear into the nearest black hole. Though he had the legal right to see me on weekends, he never bothered most times. Mom would have understood if I had other plans that didn't involve seeing my father. She might have even taken my side when I blew him off. Suddenly, I lost my appetite. I put the rest of the food away.

6: THE DJINN

When Monday rolled around, I was a zombie. The stress of the weekend had taken a toll on me. I shambled off the bus and headed to the school, barely able to stop yawning. Dylan waited for me outside the main doors.

"You look like me after a marathon of Super Mario. What happened?"

"Shut up, Dylan. I don't want to talk about it."

"Chill, Kristina. I think my head is rolling around somewhere."

"Sorry. How are you feeling?"

"In spite of being paralyzed for a few hours, not bad. Still a little stiff from the after effects, but I'm feeling a lot better than you look."

"Har har."

Classes did nothing to improve my mood. In Mr. Carlton's language arts class, I had to prop my hands under my chin so I didn't fall asleep as he droned on about *Shoeless Joe*, a baseball novel about a guy who ploughed under his cornfield so he could build a diamond for ghosts of baseball players.

"When Ray Kinsella completed the field, the ghosts came, just like the voice promised. Who do you think is the voice?"

The room went dead silent. I was hoping the ghost voice from the novel might answer for us.

Mr. Carlton sighed. "Did anyone here even read the chapters I assigned last week?"

More silence. Ask an obvious question; get an obvious answer.

"Well, then it looks like you're going to have more homework for tonight."

Groans of protest filled the room.

"Can't we just watch the movie?" one of the girls at the back of the class asked. "My brother said he watched it when they studied the novel. It's about the same thing, isn't it?"

"Well, you just earned the class a new assignment. For tomorrow, I want you all to give me three paragraphs summarizing the book. And if I see anything that looks remotely like a Wikipedia entry, you get an automatic fail. Get started."

More groans.

"Oh, you'd rather write four paragraphs? Is that what I'm hearing?"

The room fell silent except for the fluttering of pages as the students began to read.

The rest of the day dragged on, but lunch

gave me the break I needed to get up to the Vault and talk to Grimoire. Dylan wanted Anji to join us, but I rejected the idea. I told him I didn't quite trust her, yet, but something else nagged me about her. Maybe it was how condescending she acted when we needed information from her. Now that she knew the location of Rebecca, she'd be insufferable.

We crept up the stairs, making sure no one saw us. When I tried to enter the code on the lock, the portal to the Vault failed to open. I tried again. Still nothing.

Dylan asked, "You sure you got the right code?"

"I know what I'm doing," I snapped. I tried the code a third time. Nothing.

Finally, Dylan pulled out the rock chip from Tabula Rasa and scrawled a message on the floor: "We're here."

Suddenly, a whoosh of air and a beam of light bathed us. The next thing I knew, we were in the Vault, face to face with Grimoire.

"The code isn't working," I said.

"I changed it," he answered.

"Why?" Dylan asked.

"I didn't want to take any chances."

"What's the new code?" I asked.

He seemed to hesitate for a second, then

gave it to us. "The Golden Ratio. One to the right, six to the left, back to the one and then to the eight."

I noted the combination, but something distracted me. A low hum. Behind me, a massive infinity symbol glowed and made the strange droning sound. It looked like a sideways eight floating in mid-air.

"What is that?" I asked.

"A Mobius Strip."

"Wow! It's like the sickest skateboard park. Can I try?" Dylan asked, reaching out to touch it.

Grimoire grabbed his hand. "Careful. Whoever gets on the Mobius Strip never gets off. I constructed it as a prison for Rebecca, if necessary. I can't afford to have her on the loose. Once she's trapped inside, it will keep her from making any more trouble."

"You're going to lock her up?" Dylan said. "Brutal."

"It's the only way to keep the artefacts safe."

"That's a bit extreme, don't you think?" I said.

"The secrets of the Vault are too important to risk having her running around!"

I shook my head. "All you have to do is change the codes so she can't get back in. End of story."

"No. She knows the Vault exists and she won't quit until she procures the Golden Fleece."

"How can you be sure?" I asked. "What if she just sells the other artefacts and disappears?"

"She won't, and I can't trust her. The secrets of the Vault are too dangerous to be unleashed."

"So your answer is to trap Rebecca like you did Niram?"

"I'm protecting the Vault, Kristina."

"You're going too far!"

"The secrets within must never be revealed until the world is ready, and I will determine when that time is. Not you or Rebecca or anyone. Now, where is Anji? We'll need her to track Rebecca."

"You're talking about taking away Rebecca's freedom. You might as well kill her."

The silence that followed made my skin crawl. It occurred to me that he might have already been considering that option.

Dylan broke the tension. "Mr. Grimoire might be right."

"What?"

"Hear me out, Kristina. She's stolen a music box to control minds, some dragon's teeth that can create an army, and a book of spells that can do who knows what. It sounds like she's preparing for war. If we don't stop her, there's no telling what she can do."

"Are you for real?"

"I just think we might want to keep her under wraps until we know for sure what her real agenda is." He shifted in front of Grimoire and fixed an intense gaze on me, shifting his eyes to the marble staircase—the way out.

"What?"

"I'm just saying we have to *protect ourselves.*" Again, he glanced over to the staircase.

Finally, I got the hint. "Okay, okay. You might be right."

Dylan smiled. "Let's get Anji and figure out where Rebecca is. We'll be back as soon as we can, Mr. Grimoire."

We headed to the marble staircase and exited the Vault. When we reappeared in the school, I pulled Dylan down the stairs and whispered. "What was that all about?"

"He's gone full paranoid. If he's going to trap Rebecca on that thing, can you imagine what he'd do to us if he thought we were going to bail? I hate the idea of spending the rest of my life trapped in a Mobius Strip or stuck in a lamp or whatever crazy cage he builds next."

The truth settled in. "You're right, Dylan."

"We should play along until we can figure out a way to leave quietly and without setting off his full-on crazy."

"Maybe he'll calm down once we get the artefacts back."

"I don't think so."

"It's our best shot of staying on his good side, Dylan. I think if we run, he's going to put us on his enemy list."

We headed to Anji's usual haunt, but she wasn't there. Dylan led me to the grade nine classroom. Still no sign of her.

"Did she come to school today?" I asked.

"I'm not sure. Maybe she's in the computer lab."

The school bell rang, signalling the end of lunch.

"We'll find her after school," I said. "Let's not be in a rush to get back to Mr. Grimoire."

"Okay. I'll meet you at the library. For sure Anji will be there after school."

I spent the rest of the day trying to concentrate in class. The lack of sleep started to catch up with me. In math class, I dozed off with my head on the coil spine of my scribbler.

The bell rang, and my head shot straight up. I glanced around the room, trying to get my bearings. The other students snickered and pointed. One boy called me *coil face*. Rubbing my forehead, I discovered a temporary groove had formed. I stared at my desk and avoided eye contact with the kids as they filed past.

Finally, I grabbed my books and left the class. When I reached the library, I peeked inside for Anji or Dylan. No sign of them. Maybe Anji had decided to go home early rather than use the free Wi-Fi at the school. Or maybe Dylan caught up to her outside of class. I waited a few more minutes, hoping they'd show up soon. A burly teen with a greasy mullet and hockey jersey lumbered toward me. He nodded as he passed.

After him, the hall cleared quickly. A few minutes later, the teachers walked out of their classrooms. I was the only one left in the school.

I wondered if Dylan had gone to the Vault without me. I climbed the stairs and entered the new code. *Whoosh.* Once inside, I scanned the room. The Mobius Strip sat in the middle of it like a reminder of what might happen to people who crossed the Keeper of the Vault. No sign of anyone.

"Mr. Grimoire? Dylan? Anyone here?"

No answer. Not only was Grimoire gone but so was the Golden Fleece. The bare pedestal stared back at me. Grimoire must have hidden the thing. I examined the smooth surface of the Mobius Strip from a safe distance, thinking about how Grimoire was going to add Rebecca to his collection. Could he see the difference between artefacts and people? My thoughts wandered to the other prisoner in the Vault: the djinn.

I shuffled to the display case with my smartphone and the lamp. I tapped on the glass and cleared my throat. "Ahem, can you hear me in there? Niram? Are you there?"

No answer. I rapped again.

"It's me. Kristina."

Nothing. This was silly. I started to walk away.

"I'm here," a female voice said. "What do you want?"

I spun back. Smoke wafted from the screen of the phone and billowed into the shape of the exotic features of the djinn that once tried to kill me. Her vivid eyes bored holes into me.

"It's been a while," I said.

"Not quite an eternity, but yes, you could say it's been some time since we last saw each other."

"I'm sorry I tricked you."

"Not many can, so you should be proud. Perhaps one day I can return the favour."

I stiffened, half expecting her to burst through the case and attack me, but I remembered the rules of the djinn. Only if I set her free could she come out, and she couldn't do anything to me until I made three wishes. I wasn't about to do that. I had learned enough from my last encounter with this devious creature. Instead, I wanted something else from her.

"You hear everything that goes on here, don't you?"

"Oh yes, I have the perfect vantage point to observe all the madness that unfolds within these walls."

"I'm curious about Mr. Grimoire and Rebecca. Why does he think she's such a threat?"

"You mean to ask why he would construct a prison for her?"

"I'm curious."

Niram cracked a smile. "You should be terrified."

"Why?"

"Grimoire is not who he seems. He protects the secrets of the Vault, even to the point where he sees enemies in friends and danger in opportunities. One day, he may even see the same in you. In fact, you sense that now, don't you?"

She was right, but I didn't want to give away too much. Niram could be using my fears to trick me into freeing her. I had to tiptoe around this conversation without setting off any verbal traps.

"What happened between the two of them?"

Niram's smoky head wafted around the inside of the display case. "Ah, you want to know why he drove her away like he did so many of his other apprentices."

"Other apprentices?"

"Your mentor is very old and he has gone through many apprentices."

"He said he wanted to step down."

"He tells everyone that, but he's never going to give up the job. Not when he has the Golden Fleece to keep him going for the rest of eternity."

My eyes widened with realization. As an immortal, Grimoire had no need for anyone to replace him. "But why does he hire apprentices?"

"Isn't it obvious?"

I shook my head.

"And I thought you were at least a little bit clever. But you're just a mortal who had a stroke of good fortune. You lack the wit to be a Keeper of the Vault."

"Then enlighten me, Niram. Tell me what's right under my nose."

"Do you know the greatest curse of being able to live forever?"

"Curse? There's nothing wrong with that. You will never die. You get to see the future and compare it to the past."

"But whom will you share it with?"

I stopped. I hadn't considered the notion. I hadn't even thought Grimoire was someone who could experience the pain of loneliness. "He wants a friend?"

"Less a friend and more a colleague. He's never been the warmest of people. All these secrets he must hide from the world. It's the hardest thing to hold a secret. You want to share it, and who better to share those secrets with than someone who will keep your secrets?"

"Then why has he gone through so many apprentices?"

Niram laughed. "He hasn't. They've just passed away. Time goes on for them, but not for him."

"So, Rebecca's the first who actually left him?"

"Now you're starting to see the picture."

"But why?"

The djinn grinned. "I could tell you, but I won't."

"Why not?"

"Because there's nothing in it for me."

"I'm not letting you out if that's what you're thinking."

She laughed. "You're learning."

I recalled how Grimoire turned the valve on the display case to shoot liquid nitrogen inside. It was his way of controlling Niram's father. I placed my hand on the crank wheel. "I could make you talk."

Her eyes narrowed. "Don't. Please."

"You mentioned something about Rebecca."

My fingers drummed on the top of the wheel.

"You wouldn't."

"One turn and things could get uncomfortable in there."

"Oh, fine. I'll tell you, then. What do I care? Rebecca received a distressing phone call from her family."

"I thought her parents were dead, and Grimoire said she no longer stayed in touch with her grandmother."

"Apparently, he was wrong. At least from what I could gather. I only heard Rebecca's end of the phone conversation, but it sounded like her grandmother was reaching out to her after many years."

"Why would she do that now?"

"I don't know for certain, but it sounded like the grandmother was ailing."

Before I could question Niram anymore, a door opened and Grimoire entered. The smoky head dissolved and floated back into the smartphone. I spun around to catch his surprised look.

"Oh, Kristina. I hadn't expected you back so soon. Where is Dylan?"

"I thought he might be here."

He shook his head.

"We were supposed to meet Anji at the school library. When he didn't show up, I thought he might have come up here.

"No, I've not seen him at all."

Was he lying? Had he already thrown Dylan into a cage somewhere in the Vault? I looked around, nervous.

"I suppose he could have come and gone," I said.

"Perhaps."

The tension between us seemed to thicken.

"I'll check the library again."

"Do you want me to accompany you?" he offered.

"No, I'm sure you're busy with the Mobius Strip."

I half-expected Grimoire to grab me and throw me on the giant ribbon before I could leave. Dylan was right about playing along. No sense in giving a paranoid man a reason to believe he was right.

The school hallways were empty. I headed down the stairs. Not even the teachers were in their classrooms. I hesitated at the bottom of the stairwell when I heard a noise in the distance. Worried about Dr. Von Himmel's Music Box, I reached into my pocket and pulled out my old earphones. Though I had no phone, I hoped the earphones could block the sound of the music box. As an extra precaution, I also cupped my hands over my ears and started down the steps.

My body ached from the tension of holding my breath and tightening my every muscle. When I reached the bottom of the staircase, I peeked down the hallway. No sign of anyone. I didn't dare remove my hands from my ears.

Then a classroom door at the far end of the hallway opened. I jumped back around the corner and waited for a few breaths then I peeked around. Dylan shambled toward me, walking mechanically, followed by Rebecca.

7: Mind Control

I retreated up the stairwell. I needed to get back to the Vault as quickly as I could. With Dylan under Rebecca's spell, he would be taking her to the entrance. I had to warn Grimoire so he could change the code and stop Dylan and Rebecca from getting in.

When I reached the fourth floor, I realized my problem immediately. To dial the combination, I needed to uncover my ears. I gingerly pulled them away, but not before I pressed the ear buds deep. I jammed them deep into my ear, but I ignored the pain, bit my lip, and started to turn the combination dial. Golden ratio. One. Six. One. Eight. I pressed one shoulder against my ear. No music, yet.

Whoosh. The vortex opened. My stomach lurched. Limbo. Then in a blink, solid ground returned under my feet. My legs quivered for a second from the adrenaline rush.

"Mr. Grimoire! Rebecca's in the school!"

The Keeper of the Vault spun around from the display case with Niram and her father. "What happened?"

"She used Dr. Von Himmel's Music Box on Dylan. I saw him in the hallway. They're coming up the stairs."

"You didn't hear the music, did you?"

I shook my head. "You have to change the safeguards before they reach the portal entrance."

Grimoire sprang into action. He zipped up the steps two and three at a time. I never thought a man of his years could be so nimble. At the top of the stairs, he reached into his jacket and fished out a brass skeleton key. He inserted the slender key into the right banister and turned it three times. A whirling vortex appeared in front of the landing. A galaxy of stars stared out from the open maw. Grimoire fiddled with the key, turning it in either direction. The vortex responded by changing from a deep purple to a light rose. It almost looked like he was changing night to day with the twist of his key.

Finally, the vortex went white and blinked out.

"There! The access points are now closed," he announced.

"What do we do about Dylan?"

"As long as Rebecca possesses the music box, he is under her spell. If we want to rescue him, we have to capture her."

"Do you have any more of that beeswax?" I asked.

Before he could answer, we both stopped. A loud screech filled the chamber. I covered my ears.

"What is that?" I shouted. "Is she breaking through?"

He jumped on the banister and slid to the bottom of the staircase then he rushed to Tabula Rasa, the large stone slate. Etchings appeared across the smooth granite surface as if an invisible scribe were marking the slate. However, the letters were backwards.

"Do you think Dylan is sending us a message?" I asked.

He stared at the writing in capital letters. The words were reversed.

Grimoire reached behind the pedestal and retrieved an ivory hand mirror. "We can only read the message with this. Tell me what it says."

He held the glass to the slate so I could read the reflected words.

"Let's trade. Apprentice for Fleece. One hour. Will wait in library."

Grimoire sucked in air. His eyes were wide with fear, something I hadn't seen in his face before.

"What do we do?" I asked. "We can't let her hurt Dylan."

"I can't let her have the Golden Fleece. The artefact belongs in the Vault."

"Why? Because you want it all to yourself?"

"What are you talking about? Do you know the havoc that would follow if this were to get out?"

"It might save the world."

"No, it would only save one person. The Golden Fleece only works on one person at a time. You can't just hack the hide into pieces and pass them out. Imagine everyone you ever knew learning about this, but you had to choose who used it first. Do you think people would wait their turn? No, there would be chaos."

"You're wrong," I said. "You're just trying to keep this all to yourself. You don't care about Dylan. Or me. Or any of your apprentices, probably!"

"I took great pains to groom Rebecca as my apprentice. Not only did I open the Vault to her, I also opened my heart. I trusted her with my life's work because I saw something that no one else did. She has a good spirit. At least, I thought she did."

"And do you trust me?"

"Kristina, the fact that you care about Dylan so much you'd risk anything to save him shows me you have what it takes to be my apprentice."

"Then if you want me, you need Dylan, too. We have to rescue him."

"There are alternatives other than giving Rebecca the Golden Fleece."

"Such as?"

He reached into his pocket and pulled out the Mason jar of beeswax. "We will wrest the music box from her and trap her on the Mobius Strip."

"The thing is, she'll see it from a mile away."

He walked to the floating infinity symbol and spread his hands. He closed them as if he were clapping in slow motion. In response, the Mobius Strip shrank to the size of a brooch and the low hum faded out. He held the tiny strip in the palm of his hand.

"We pin this on Rebecca, and she won't trouble us ever again."

I eyed the brooch. If it was a choice between Rebecca and Dylan, I had to choose my friend. I reluctantly nodded.

"Apply the wax in your ears and we'll get going."

"Wait a minute. We can't just confront her head-on. She could order Dylan to hurt himself. We need to distract her."

"What do you have in mind?"

"Is there a way we can disguise something to look like the Golden Fleece? What about Blackwell's Phantasm Ball?"

He beamed. "Brilliant. Subterfuge."

Grimoire walked over to a display case and retrieved the large crystal ball.

"The Golden Fleece," he announced as he shook the artefact. Instantly his hands were filled with shimmering gold.

"Great. So this will buy us enough time to get close to Rebecca and grab the music box."

"No. We have to pin the Mobius Strip on her first. Then we can take the box."

"I'm not taking any chances," I said. "We have to save Dylan first."

"She can't be allowed to escape again."

"If I can get the box, I'll turn the crank and she'll be under my control," I said. "And Dylan, too. That's how it works, right?"

"Whoever hears the music will answer the bidding of whoever turns the music box crank last. But we don't know what other surprises she has for us. Best to put the Mobius Strip on her."

"Okay. Let's do this." I slathered the beeswax into my ears while Grimoire scooped a dollop and jammed it into his ear.

"I'm ready!" I shouted.

"What?"

I signalled a thumbs up. He nodded and pointed to the marble staircase. We climbed the stairs. Grimoire handed me the fake Golden Fleece and fished out his key. He turned it three times and the vortex appeared. He jumped through and I followed.

We appeared on the landing of the fourth floor. Grimoire pointed at the combination lock and flashed his fingers at me, close to his chest. *Five, eight, zero, seven.* I nodded to signal I understood the new combination code.

He took the Golden Fleece back and we headed down the stairs. I glanced around the hallways for any sign of people. Even the custodian was nowhere to be seen. Odd. Mrs. Gavinder should have been working by now. I wanted to tell Grimoire about my concerns, but of course he couldn't hear me.

On the main level of the school, a broom lay across on the floor. We stepped over it and headed to the library. I checked over my shoulder in case anyone had plans of sneaking up behind us. The hallway was clear. I pressed my body against the wall so no one could see us through the library window. I pushed Grimoire back with one hand as I peeked through the window.

Dylan sat ramrod straight at one of the tables. Beside him, Rebecca absently turned the crank on Dr. Von Himmel's Music Box, but my beeswax blocked the sound. I signalled to Grimoire that I was going in. He nodded and followed me.

Rebecca cracked a sly smile and waved at

the empty chairs at the table. I shook my head and replied, "Send us Dylan and we'll give you the Golden Fleece."

She mouthed something at me. I didn't hear anything, but I shook my head as if I didn't agree with anything she said.

"Dylan first. We'll leave the Golden Fleece at the door for you." I nudged Grimoire.

The Vault Keeper held up the fake Golden Fleece. Rebecca's eyes fixated on the glistening hide in his hands. He began to advance on her, angling himself to the right while I took a few steps to the left, trying to flank her. My attention was so focused on the music box I didn't see the figure emerging from between the bookshelves right away.

Anji!

She swung a baseball bat at my head. I ducked just in time. The bat rang against the metal shelves. I backed away as the after-school goon with the mullet appeared from the other aisle, brandishing a hockey stick. Dylan rose from the table, also wielding a hockey stick.

I grabbed Grimoire and gestured toward the attackers. He nodded and motioned me to head toward the door. When I turned around, my heart sank at the sight. Mrs. Gavinder was blocking my escape. She held a screwdriver as if it were a knife.

"We're trapped," I yelled, but Grimoire couldn't hear me.

I grabbed books on the counter and hurled them at Mrs. Gavinder. She swatted them away. Then I grabbed a dictionary and hurled it at Dylan. The heavy book landed in front of him.

Grimoire shouted something as he ran toward me. I tossed another book at Mrs. Gavinder. She dodged the book but not Grimoire. He barrelled into her and slammed her against the wall. She slumped to the ground trying to catch her breath while he fled from the library.

I started after him, but hands grabbed me from behind.

8: The Golden Fleece

The two boys held me fast. I tried to pull free, but they had a firm grip on both my arms. I tried kicking at their legs. No luck. Rebecca mouthed something I couldn't make out. I shook my head. She turned to Anji and barked instructions.

Anji walked toward me and reached for my ears. I angled my head away, but she was faster. She dug her fingers into my right ear and scraped out the beeswax. The yellow substance clung to the end of her fingers like dried snot.

Sound rushed back into one ear and I could hear myself screaming. "Let me go!"

Rebecca crossed her arms over her chest. "I had a feeling you might try to double-cross me, so I decided to get some insurance. Get her other ear."

Anji obeyed and scraped the wax out of my left ear, then she stepped back so I had a clear view of the music box on the table. Rebecca picked up the device and put one hand on the golden crank.

"Dylan and Anji, hold onto your friend. The rest of you, bring me back the Golden Fleece. I don't care what you do to get it."

Mrs. Gavinder and the mullet goon left the library. Dylan shifted himself over and hooked one of my arms behind my back. Anji grabbed the other arm and pulled it back. Pain in my shoulder blades erupted from the force of their holds.

"Now, let's see about making you a little more obedient," Rebecca said, smiling.

"No, wait! You do that and you'll never see Mr. Grimoire or the Golden Fleece again."

She hesitated. "He's not going to lose his new apprentices."

"You think we matter to him? You know he locked up the Golden Fleece and hid it the moment he knew you were coming after it. He even hid it from us. I didn't see it until now."

Rebecca's fingers twitched on the crank. She bit her lower lip for a second.

"He abandoned me in the library with you. That's how much he thinks of me. You believe he's going to trade? He replaced you quickly and he'll replace Dylan and me just as quickly."

She took another step forward. "I don't believe you."

"You know him better than I do. What do you think is true?"

She lowered the box, unsure.

I drove myself backwards, slamming Dylan

and Anji against the hard wood of the library counter. Dylan gasped for air and let go of my arm. Anji clung onto me, but I kicked her shins and pulled away.

I lunged for the music box. I smacked hard into Rebecca, sending the artefact tumbling through the air. She lay sprawled on the floor, while I dove to catch the music box and crawled forward to where it landed a few feet away.

She howled. "Don't let her take it!"

Anji leapt over me and knocked the box beyond my reach, then stepped on my wrist. Pain shot up my arm. I tried to yank back, but she ground her heel into my flesh. I screamed.

As Rebecca staggered toward the artefact, I drove my free hand into the back of Anji's knee, causing her leg to buckle. I pulled my other hand free and shoved her to the ground. She landed in front of Rebecca, slowing her down enough for me to dive for the music box. I scrambled to my feet as Dylan charged at me.

"Get her!" Rebecca yelled.

I backed up, fumbling for the crank. I moved behind a table, trying to buy myself time, but my back slammed against the bookshelf. My trembling fingers gripped the smooth brass handle. I tried to spin the crank, but it wouldn't turn. I panicked as Dylan closed the gap. I tried again and again.

Finally, I realized I was turning it the wrong way. I reversed the crank, and the music box lid popped open. Tinny, toy piano music tinkled out of the box, with a minor chord that grated on one's nerves. Dylan screeched to a halt.

"Sit down," I ordered. "You too, Anji. Crisscross, apple sauce."

They plopped on the floor like obedient kindergarten kids.

On the other side of the library, my enemy wavered on her feet.

"Rebecca, stay right where you are!"

She stopped swaying.

"Have a seat at the table with me." She obeyed without question. The sudden rush of power both thrilled and terrified me. I could tell her to do anything I wanted. Right now, I needed information.

"Rebecca, you are under my command. You must tell me the truth. Do you understand?"

"Yes."

"Where are the artefacts you stole?"

"They are in my grandmother's house."

"What were you planning to do with them?"

"I needed to sell them to make money."

"So, this was all just a get-rich-quick plan?"

"No. My grandmother is dying. She has stage-four breast cancer. The doctors have tried to treat her in Edmonton, but nothing is working."

"Oh," That made me stop for a moment. "Um, I'm sorry about your grandmother. That's why you were trying to get the Golden Fleece, wasn't it?"

"Yes, but Grimoire caught me, and I had to find another way to save my grandmother. I found a drug that might help. It's called Palbociclib, and it's being used in clinical trials. My grandmother was too old to be accepted, but she could get the drug in the States if I could fly her down there."

"Mr. Grimoire said you had a falling out with her. Why are you going to all this trouble?"

"Yes, but she's still my grandmother."

"I would do anything for my Lao Lao. What happened, Rebecca?"

"I never knew my parents before they died. I only knew them from the stories my grandmother told me. I knew them from the photos she kept. But when I grew older, she started to call me by the wrong name. She mistook me for my mother. Said I looked exactly like her. I hated it. I didn't want to be reminded of the woman who died."

"And that's when you ran away, isn't it?"

She nodded. "The more I tried to push her away, the more she tried to pull me in. Grimoire was the first person to treat me like I was my own person."

"What changed? Why did you reach out to her now?"

She looked down at the table. "I didn't. She tracked me down to tell me she had a month to live. When I heard her voice, nothing else mattered. She wanted to see me one last time. I hated myself for running away. Over the dumbest thing. Now, I want to get back the time we lost."

I cringed. Her story sounded all too familiar. I shook off the guilt.

"My grandmother is all I have left in the world," she said. "I would do anything to save her."

I drummed my fingers on the table and glanced up at the door. Now that I had possession of the music box, the spell would have worn off of the people chasing Grimoire. He could be making his way back any moment with the Mobius Strip. If I was going to act, I had to do it now.

"Dylan, find Mr. Grimoire and bring him to the library. Tell him we are here."

He stood and headed out of the library. I waited until he was gone then I turned to Rebecca and Anji. "Get up and come with me."

They obeyed. I headed back to the portal where I instructed the girls to look away as I entered the new code for the access. The next thing I knew we were standing in the Vault.

"Listen to me carefully, Rebecca, I'm going to give you the Golden Fleece, but you have to show me where the other artefacts you stole are in exchange and give them to me."

"I hid them in my grandmother's house in the vegetable cellar. They are in a locked metal box. The key is here." She fished a brass key out of her pocket and handed it to me. "Now where is the Golden Fleece?"

The pedestal for the artefact was bare. In the rush to capture Rebecca, I had forgotten that Grimoire had hidden the real Golden Fleece. A wave of panic started from my toes and rolled up my legs. It wouldn't take long for the Keeper of the Vault to return once he saw we weren't in the library. I had to find the Golden Fleece now, but I didn't know the Vault's secrets.

"Do you know where he would have hidden the Golden Fleece?" I asked Rebecca.

She shook her head.

"We can't waste any time. Start looking for it," I ordered.

Anji and Rebecca split to cover one end of the Vault while I hurried through the collection on the other side. I stopped at the display case that contained my smartphone and Niram.

Could I trust her? I had no other choice. I rapped on the glass.

"Niram, come out."

Blue smoke billowed from the screen and morphed into the head of the djinn. She glanced around the room, spotting Rebecca. "I see you've made a new friend."

"I have no time. You know where the Golden Fleece is, don't you?"

"Indeed, I do."

"Tell me."

Her eyes twinkled. "No."

I gritted my teeth. I hated her smug grin. "I don't have time to negotiate."

I held up the music box. "I can make you tell me."

She laughed. "Go ahead and try. The music box only works on humans."

I put down the box and grabbed the crank wheel on the side of the display case instead. "Want me to make things chilly for you, Niram?"

Her eyes widened, but she cracked a smarmy grin. "You can torture me, but I don't think you have enough time to force me to tell you. I suspect time is not your friend right now."

I started to turn the wheel. Hiss. Liquid nitrogen shot into the case. Niram's head shrieked.

"Tell me," I ordered.

"Y-y-you w-won't get me to t-t-alk in t-t-time."

She was right. Grimoire would be coming back

here any minute. I spun the wheel the other way, shutting off the cloud of cold air.

Niram's teeth chattered. "M-much better."

"I can't let you out," I said.

"Oh, I'm no longer interested in that."

"What do you mean?"

"My father and I are enjoying our newfound time together. He's told me stories about his adventures before I was created. They are incredible. I'm having the best time."

"Really? Lucky you. Wish I could say the same about my dad."

"You do not get along with your father?"

"No. He treats me like I'm some kind of toy that he's outgrown."

"That is unfortunate. I'm sorry."

"It's not your problem. I'm glad you have a good relationship, and I'm glad I could help you. Now will you show me where the Golden Fleece is?"

"No." She smiled. "There is one thing, however, that would make everything perfect."

"What?" I asked, fearing the worst.

"I used to be able to browse through the world within your device. I could see anything I wanted, but now I can't."

"You can't get on the Internet."

"No, I wanted to show my father how the

world is now, but my words aren't enough. I need to show him."

"When I gave up the phone, I had to cancel the data plan. You won't be able to connect at all."

"Then restore the plan."

"I'm sorry, Niram, but I just can't do that. The plan is cancelled and even if I could reconnect it, I don't have the money to pay for it."

"Then you won't ever find the Golden Fleece," she threatened.

I glanced at the entry point in the Vault. No sign of Grimoire, yet. "Please, Niram. I'll tell you what. When I get a new phone, I'll visit you and your father every week and let you browse the Internet, and until I get my new phone, I'll let you use Dylan's phone."

Niram cocked her head to one side. "You would make the time for me?"

I nodded. "In case you get sick of talking to your dad."

She laughed. "I'm not sick of him, yet."

"Do we have a deal?"

She winked. A loud pop startled me. A glow filled the chamber from the bare pedestal, but now it was no longer bare. The Golden Fleece was mounted on it as if it had always been there.

"What? How?"

"Out of sight, out of mind. Grimoire cast a

spell of invisibility. He really should soundproof the display case because I'm a terrible snoop."

"Thank you, Niram," I said.

"Don't forget our arrangement."

"I won't." I was amazed she wanted her father's company—not something I could ever imagine.

I lifted the ram's hide from the pedestal. Though large, the Fleece barely weighed more than a helium balloon, and the hide felt warm against my skin. I wanted to wrap myself in the soft fur, but I resisted the urge.

"I have it," I yelled. "Get over here."

The girls joined me.

"You have the Golden Fleece," Rebecca said.

I hugged the pelt to my chest, never wanting to let it go. "I'll hang on to this until we get to your grandmother's house. Where is she?"

"She's resting at her home. The hospital can't do anything more for her, and she'd rather be where she feels comfortable."

"Okay. We're going to see her, give her the Golden Fleece, and let it do its magic. Once you give me the stuff you stole, you're going to disappear. Get as far away from the Vault as you can and never come back. Grimoire plans on making you a permanent part of the collection, and I can't let that happen. You're going to forget the Vault ever existed and go on with your life. Understand?"

"Yes," she said. "Thank you."

"Follow me." We headed up the marble staircase and stepped off the landing. We reappeared in the school and ran down the steps to the third floor. I stopped. Footsteps echoed from below.

Grimoire's voice boomed: "Dylan, you are sure Kristina said she was in the library?"

"She said to bring you to the library. You must come with me, sir."

"No, we're going to the Vault. Something is wrong."

"No, we have to go to the library. Kristina said I had to bring you there."

"We already went. Now let go of my arm."

Dylan was still acting on my last orders. It would buy me some time—not a lot. I motioned Rebecca and Anji to follow me down the hallway to the other stairwell. We crept down the steps and out of the school.

"Rebecca, take me to your grandmother's house," I ordered.

She jogged across the street. Ahead, Grimoire's ugly yellow Volkswagen bug waited for us. She hopped into the driver's side and opened the passenger door for Anji and me. We jumped in as she started the car. I fastened my seatbelt as she pulled away from the curb and sped down the street toward the north end of the city.

In the side-view mirror, the downtown buildings shrank as we got farther and farther away. I tried to make note of where we were in case I had to find my way back. The only familiar landmark was a traffic circle. We zipped around and drove east toward the hockey arena where the Oilers used to play. The car rolled past the building, which always reminded me of a giant stack of pancakes.

We arrived in a neighbourhood lined with old trees and modest bungalows built in an era long before I was born. Rebecca turned right onto a street and rolled up two blocks before stopping in front of a small house with a makeshift wooden ramp at the front entrance. The lights in the living room were on.

We climbed out of the car, and I took the keys from Rebecca before following her up the ramp.

"Rebecca, remember your orders. Get me the stolen artefacts. Once we cure your grandmother, you disappear for good and forget everything."

"Yes."

"Anji, keep an eye on her. Make sure she doesn't try to run away."

"I will watch her."

The rancid odour of a full bedpan made me shudder the instant we entered the house. A frail woman, hooked up to an IV, slept peacefully in a bed in the middle of the living room.

"Grandma," Rebecca whispered. "Where's the nurse? She was supposed to stay here until I got back."

The woman opened her eyes. "Betty. Oh my. Is that you?"

"No, Grandma. It's Rebecca."

"Right, right. Becky. I'm sorry."

"It's okay." Rebecca grabbed her grandmother's hand. The old woman's ring stared back at me. The diamonds on the setting formed a tiny star.

"I'm sorry."

"It's okay. Where's the nurse?"

"She had to step out for some fresh air. I told her I'd be fine for a while."

Judging by the smell, I could see why the nurse stepped out.

The old woman turned her head to eye me. "Who are they?"

"I'm a friend," I answered. "I brought something to keep you warm."

Rebecca's grandmother smiled. "Aren't you sweet?" she rasped. "I am feeling a bit chilly, my dear. What is your name?"

"Kristina."

"Call me Nancy, dear."

"Can I put this on you?" I asked.

She coughed. "Yes. I'd like that."

I laid the Golden Fleece over her thin body, making sure the ram's head was at her feet.

"Rebecca, please go get those things we talked about."

She hesitated for a second, her eyes on her grandmother.

"Anji, go with her and make sure she doesn't try anything funny."

The two girls left the room.

"This blanket you brought me is so warm," Nancy said.

"It has that effect on people," I replied.

We sat quietly for a moment, but I hate awkward silences.

"You must be glad to have Rebecca back in your life."

She smiled, pulling the Golden Fleece up around her chin. "I couldn't be happier. I'm so glad that I found her again."

"How were you able to track her down?"

"The nurse that helps me is good with that computer. She said she could track down Rebecca for me."

"Did Rebecca tell you anything about what she's doing now?"

"Something about a museum. No, now she's gone into business for herself. She always was a go-getter. Just like her mother."

"Yes, she is."

"How do you know her?"

"I work at the...museum where she used to work."

Nancy pulled her hand out from under the Golden Fleece. The diamond star twinkled. "Be careful, dear. Rebecca said she had an awful time working there."

"Really? Why?"

"She hated her boss. Said he was too controlling." She shifted under the Golden Fleece, sitting up in the bed.

"How are you feeling, Nancy?"

"I think my appetite is coming back."

"Do you want me to get you something?"

"Oh no, I'll get the nurse to bring me the sandwich she made earlier."

She shifted again. The weight of the ram's head caused the Golden Fleece to slide off. I put the music box on the bed and readjusted the pelt.

"Such a pretty box," Nancy said.

I straightened up and tried to stop her, but she started to turn the crank. "No!"

A single note played.

9: Face the Music

A fog began to cloud my mind. I had to act fast. Before Nancy could utter a word, I grabbed the music box and turned the crank. The tinny music played, and my brain fog lifted. An icicle of dread knifed my belly. Rebecca was free. I rotated the crank, hoping she could hear the music. Nancy stiffened, her eyes turning vacant.

"Stay here. Do not move until I get back."

"I will, dear."

I headed toward the back of the house, cranking the music box to broadcast the melody. The hallway was empty. Outside the back door, a large woman stiffened, falling under my control. The nurse. I rounded the corner and stared down the steps. A bare light bulb illuminated the basement storage area. I headed down.

At the bottom of the stairs, I called out. "Rebecca, come to me now. Bring the artefacts."

No response. I checked the laundry room. Empty.

"Anji, can you hear me? Don't let Rebecca get away."

The spare room was next. A bed with a daisy

quilt sat in the middle. I turned on the light and entered the room. A pair of legs jutted out from the other side of the bed. I crept closer. Anji lay on the carpeted floor, knocked out. I rushed to check on her, but behind me, the closet rattled. I spun around and cranked the music box. "Come out, Rebecca."

Nothing. I slid my hand into the crack between the sliding door and the wall.

Suddenly, she burst out, howling. Our bodies crashed together, and she shoved me on the bed. A pair of noise-cancelling headphones was clamped over her ears.

I tried to claw the headphones off with one hand, but she smacked the music box out of my other hand. I punched her in the chin, knocking her back. She rolled off the bed and ran to the closet where she grabbed a department store shopping bag.

I jumped off the bed and intercepted her as she reached the doorway. My shoulder slammed into her, driving her into the jamb. The paper bag fell to the floor and its contents spilled out.

My gaze shifted to the book and Dragon's Teeth on the tiled floor. Rebecca's elbow clipped me on the side of the head. Dazed, I reeled back.

She sprinted up the steps.

"Stop the woman running out of the house,"

I yelled, hoping the nurse would hear.

I raced up the stairs to the back porch, where Rebecca had knocked the nurse down. She sprinted to the fence. She scaled the fence with the ease of a mountain climber. I ran across the yard and tried to haul myself up, but a pair of hands grabbed me.

The nurse.

"Let go of me!"

She did.

"What are you doing? Why did you stop me?"

"You told me to stop the woman running. You were running."

I growled then climbed to the top of the fence. No sign of Rebecca. The alley was empty except for a black cat that scurried under a neighbour's fence. The nurse and I returned to the living room where Nancy rested under the Golden Fleece. Her cheeks were pink as health was returning to her body.

"How are you feeling, Nancy?" I asked.

"I feel as if I could do a dozen push-ups."

"That's good. I think the Golden Fleece has worked. I'm going to take this back from you now. I want both of you to close your eyes and wait until you hear me leave. As soon as the door closes, you will forget everything about our meeting. When you wake up, you won't remember anything about what happened here. Do you understand?"

The nurse nodded. Nancy smiled. "I will forget. It was so nice to meet you, Kristina."

"I'm glad to have met you as well." I gathered up the Golden Fleece and headed downstairs to free Anji.

"Sorry, the music changed and before I knew I had control of myself, Rebecca jumped me."

"Don't worry about it, Anji. We got what we came here for."

We collected the artefacts in the shopping bag.

"You know, I heard you talking to that creature in the Vault," Anji said. "About your dad and how you don't get along."

"That's none of your business," I said shortly.

"Divorce?" she asked.

"Just grab the stuff and let's go."

We scooped up the artefacts and headed out of the house.

"Join the club. At first, you think it's going to be cool with two birthday parties and two gifts, but then it turns out to be no birthday parties because your parents are too busy arguing about who gets you which weekend to remember."

"Did your dad take off on you?"

She shrugged. "Yeah, but I didn't care." She opened the car door.

"Do you ever see him?"

"I get the obligatory birthday card. Maybe a text on the weekends he's supposed to visit me. Not much face to face."

"Doesn't it bother you?"

Anji shook her head. "Get in. I'll drive."

"There is no way you have your driver's licence," I protested.

"I won't tell if you won't."

"Might be better if we took the bus. Last thing I want is for these artefacts to end up in a police station."

"Suit yourself." She headed toward the main street at the end of the block.

"My dad wants back into my life, but I don't know if he's going to stick around," I confessed.

"Do you want him to?" Anji asked.

"Yes. No. I'm not sure."

"That's your problem. You're letting him tie you up in knots. You can't control what he does, but he's got you stuck in a loop."

"How did you learn to deal with it?" I asked.

She scanned the street then shuffled toward a bus stop across the road. "If my dad didn't want to be part of my life, I couldn't make him come back. But I also wasn't going to let it change me. The less I worried about him showing up, the better I felt. Plus, I might have faked some bad online reviews of his restaurant. You can't purge all the bitterness out."

I cracked a smile. "I like the revenge part."

"We all do. But it only helps for a little while."

Back at the Vault, Dylan had recovered from the effects of the music box, but Grimoire was still trying to get over what I had done. The veins in his forehead nearly burst through his skin as he yelled and stomped around the Vault. I was tempted to use the music box to calm him down.

"Explain to me why you thought it was a good idea to give the Golden Fleece to the very person who tried to steal it in the first place. Tell me what twisted logic helped you come up with this very notion, Kristina."

"She was under the control of the music box," I said. "She had to do everything I told her. So I told her to tell me the truth. When she did, I decided we should help her grandmother."

"That was not your decision to make. You are not the Keeper of the Vault."

"She did get everything back," Anji said in my defense.

I opened the department store shopping bag

and tipped it over. The contents spilled out—Aleister Crowley's *Book of Spells*, Dr. Himmel's music box, the Dragon's Teeth and the Golden Fleece.

"Amazing!" Grimoire shouted. "They're all here."

"Oh, and this, too." I tossed the car keys on top of the pile.

"You found my car?"

"Might as well be one of these antiques. It's old enough. We left it at Rebecca's grandmother's house."

Dylan jumped in. "That's fantastic, Kristina. What about my phone?"

"You mean this?" Anji said, fishing Dylan's phone and charger out of her pocket.

"Awesome! Look, Mr. Grimoire. They recovered everything. That's something to cheer about."

"Except you brought Rebecca here," Grimoire huffed. "She would have seen the new security measures."

"You can change them again," Anji suggested. "I could help you. I'm good at coming up with unbreakable passwords."

"She's a whiz at that kind of stuff," Dylan agreed. "Maybe set up a trap, so the codes to enter the place will send Rebecca into some kind of limbo prison."

I shook my head. "I don't think she'll be coming back, now that her grandmother is better."

Grimoire still fumed. "This doesn't change the fact that you risked one of the most valuable collections in the Vault. And for what?"

"Rebecca gets to have her grandmother back. That's all she wanted in the first place. She was willing to risk everything to save someone she cared about. Isn't that what you said you wanted in an apprentice?"

He said nothing, but his dour expression softened.

"Rebecca's grandmother was the only family she's known. Why wouldn't I help her?"

"When the doctors find out how her grandmother got better, they are going to want to see the cure," he said.

"Well, she won't be able to tell them anything because I told her to forget the whole story. The music box has its charms."

Dylan smiled. "Kristina did what you wanted, sir. Her methods might not be the ones you would have used, but she got the job done. Isn't that the only thing that matters?"

Grimoire fell silent, glaring at us.

Finally, he sighed. "Very well. I'll admit I'm relieved the artefacts are back, but we are going to have a serious discussion about how to maintain the security of the Vault in the future. I expect things to be done in a particular fashion and I don't like any deviations."

I nodded. "I think we've figured that out by now."

"Yes. Well. Let's get these items back to their rightful places," he said. "I believe the Dragon's Teeth were arranged in the Chinese symbol for power. And the book—"

Anji checked her phone. "Uh, actually, I have to get home before my parents kill me."

"Oh, right," Grimoire said. "Sometimes I forget you have lives outside of here."

Dylan and I shared a look. I hoped the old man would let us leave in peace. My friend didn't wait. He led Anji to the staircase.

"You going to be okay on your own, Mr. Grimoire?" I asked, pretending to be helpful.

"Oh yes. Of course. Many things to do. Not much time to do it in." He picked up the Golden Fleece, then turned to me and smiled. "I'm sorry about earlier. The collection is all that I have. I can't afford to lose any of it."

He returned to fussing over the exact location to place the Fleece, almost as if to place it anywhere else would shatter the careful world he had built.

It occurred to me that this Vault was the

only world he knew now. Rebecca's betrayal had threatened his life's work, his way of thinking, and his reason for existing. Any change in his world would be scary.

He looked so tiny among the collection and so lonely in the vast room. I suddenly felt sorry for him. But how could I judge? I was exactly like him—a person who refused to allow change in her life.

The following weekend, I was supposed to get together with Dad again for our family time. This time, my suitcase was packed when he showed up. He flashed a quizzical glance at Mom. "Did you get her ready?"

"I'm old enough to pack my own suitcase, Dad."

"Sorry. I didn't mean anything by that. Shall we go?"

"Yeah."

"I'll bring her back Sunday."

"Sure," Mom said. "Make it after supper. I have a study group that day."

"Is that okay with you, Kristina?" he asked.

"Thanks for asking, Dad. It'll be fine."

When we got in his car, he didn't start it up right away. Instead, he reached behind the seat and pulled out a white box.

"Your mother said you lost your phone. I thought the least I could do for you is get you this."

He handed me the box containing a brand new smartphone.

"Are you serious, Dad?"

"Figure it might be easier for me to get a hold of you this way, rather than leaving messages on the home line. We could do some text talking."

"Dad, it's just *texting*."

"I know. J.K. Your old man isn't that old."

I smiled.

"Go ahead. Open it. I've already programmed my number in speed dial."

I lifted the cover from the box. Inside, the screen of my brand new phone gleamed. My grudge against Dad was still pretty raw, but I didn't want to turn into Grimoire, who let one betrayal shape his entire impression of Rebecca. I thought about how Rebecca gave her grandmother a second chance.

"Well?" Dad asked.

I let go of the anger for just a second. "It's not bad."

He beamed. "I'm glad you like it. I know how

these things are like a third arm for kids these days."

"You don't know the half of it, Dad."

"So what do you want to do, Kristina?"

Instead of a grunt, I gave him a real answer: "I packed a sweater so I could keep warm. We could go to the Chinese Garden. I could tell you the story about why the rat is the first on the Chinese calendar. If you think that's something you'd like to do."

His eyes widened with surprise and I could see him try to control the grin that threatened to take over his whole face. "I'd like that very much."

Epilogue

A week had passed, and life had returned to normal at school. Dylan ribbed me for taking control over him every chance he had. "What is your bidding, my mistress?"

"I want you to pay for my data plan."

"I will do so with empty promises and the excuse that I'm broke."

We debated whether or not to return to the Vault. Dylan wanted to stay away, but I had an urge to go back. Anji also wanted to go. She was curious about the artefacts and she wanted to help set up Grimoire's new security system. Between the two of us, we convinced Dylan to return.

"He seemed to calm down once he had the artefacts back. Maybe the stress of losing them made him lose his common sense," Anji said.

"You want to take that chance?"

"Come on, Dylan," I said. "We're the only ones who can say we've met a djinn and seen real magic. You want to give that up?"

"I guess not."

"We'll just visit. If he still seems unstable,

we'll get out and never go back. Okay?"

"I still don't know."

I hummed a few bars of the music box melody. "You must do what I tell you."

"Yes, master," Anji droned.

Dylan laughed. "Okay. Okay. I'll go. Just no more humming. You two are terrible."

At the fourth floor landing, I pulled out the Tabula Rasa rock chip and scrawled a message on the floor. "We are here."

We waited for a few minutes then a flash of light came from behind the doors. Through the windows, the Vault had appeared. Grimoire had changed the way in. He opened the doors and ushered us inside.

"You are well rested, I trust."

"Yes," I replied.

"Love what you did to the place," Dylan said. "It seems so secure now."

"You can tell?"

"He's joking, sir."

"Ah, I see. Droll. We have to go back to Rebecca's grandmother's house."

"Why?" Anji asked. "We got your car back. Don't tell me the muffler fell off the old thing."

"I was looking over Aleister Crowley's *Book of Spells* yesterday, and I noticed it's missing some pages."

I stiffened. "Are you sure?"

He nodded. "Definitely."

"What were the pages about?" Dylan asked.

"I believe they contained a spell to summon a creature."

"What kind of creature?"

"One we don't want to meet."

I chewed my bottom lip. "Do you think Rebecca took them out of the book?"

"She might have, but I'm hoping the pages fell out at the house. The binding is rather fragile. Perhaps we should return to her grandmother's house and search for the pages."

Moments later, the four of us piled into Grimoire's tiny car and inched at turtle speed toward the house where we had last encountered Rebecca. Anji had dropped a GPS pin for the house on her smartphone and guided us to the location.

Next door to the house, a neighbour raked leaves from his lawn. Grimoire waved at him, while I covered my face in case he might have seen me last night. I went to the door and rang the bell. No answer. I knocked. Nothing.

Anji peered through the picture window. "Last night, I thought we could see her bed in the living room from here."

"I don't see anything," Dylan said, cupping his hand over his eyes.

"Can I help you folks?" the neighbour with the rake asked.

Grimoire answered. "Yes, I'm an old acquaintance of Nancy Collins, and I was hoping to catch up with her."

"Nancy? I'm afraid she's not here anymore."

"Where did she go?" Anji asked.

The neighbour lowered his voice. "She had cancer. I think she went somewhere for treatment."

"Then who is living here now?" I asked.

"A new renter. She moved in a couple of months ago now."

I stiffened. *A couple of months?* "Do you happen to know her name?"

"A real nice lady. Lenore... Lenore... Frobisher. Yeah, that's it."

Grimoire flashed a look at me. He also recognized the name. Lenore Frobisher was the collector who wanted to buy the Vault artefacts.

"Is Mrs. Frobisher around?" Grimoire asked.

The neighbour pulled off his trucker hat and scratched his head. "Not since last week. Looked like she was headed on vacation or something."

"Thanks," Grimoire said before ushering the three of us back to the car.

Once inside the vehicle, he turned to us. "This can't be good. It would seem that Rebecca might be in league with Lenore Frobisher.

I shook my head. "She was under the spell of the music box. She had to tell me the truth, and she said this woman was her grandmother," I said. "There's no way she could have lied."

"Then Lenore must have duped Rebecca," Grimoire said.

"What did she want?" Dylan asked. "Was it the pages? Or was there something else in the stolen artefacts?"

The unanswered questions gave me shivers.

TO BE CONTINUED...

Keepers of the Vault: Fire and Glass

The adventure begins...

MARTY CHAN

Marty Chan writes books for kids and plays for adults. He's best known for his Marty Chan Mystery series. When he's not writing, he's practising stage magic for his school presentations. For more information, please visit martychan.com.

Read an interview with Marty about the Keepers of the Vault series at clockwisepress.com.